THE ACCUSED

THE ACCUSED

John Woods

Woods publishing   Tucson, Arizona

This edition was prepared for publication by
Ghost River Images
5350 East Fourth Street
Tucson, Arizona 85711
www.ghostriverimages.com

ISBN 978-1-7338435-3-9

Library of Congress Control Number: 2019907232

Printed in the United States of America
June 2019

Contents

Dedication

For Bunker de France

Thanks Bunker. Couldn't have done it without you.

Chapter One—In the Beginning

It's easy to accuse those that are different and Max Brauny was definitely different.

Young Max was six years old and lived on the third floor on West Tenth Street in New York City. Tony, who was twelve and lived on the second floor, said, "Max, my daddy says you and your momma, each of you are about twice as wide as anyone else in the world. He said, your faces are about halfway between what the Neanderthal and what the modern man looks like. You're a neat kid Max, but you and your Momma, you sure are different."

He asked his mother about that.

She paused, looked at the boy, nodded, and said, "We are different . . . and by my standards you are the neatest, most beautiful six year old kid in the whole world. I am the heaviest boned and the strongest woman on the face of the earth and you, my son, are the heaviest boned and strongest six year old kid in the whole world. We are special, unique, and there are no others like us anywhere."

"Why?"

"Because we are, we just are. There hasn't been more than one other like us for probably the last 50,000 years. When you get older I'll tell you more. Now get dressed. I need to get you to your first day of school and then I'm due in Court."

• • •

Max's mother, as an infant, had been abandoned on a church doorstep. Ed Brauny and wife Edith, an older couple, having lost their daughter and grandchild in an auto accident, and living the relaxed but now an empty retired life up in Putnam County, learning of this little girl that no one wanted, watched and saw that this child was alert, animated and gregarious. The Braunys adopted this different little girl and named her Alexis Brauny.

As a child and hiding behind her exuberance, Lexi was watching and evaluating.

With the advance of puberty, Lexi's hips spread, she developed a good bust and exchanged gender neutral clothing for tight slacks that showed off her new female figure.

With the arrival of puberty it became obvious that it was young women that caught Lexi's eye. This did not trouble her, nor did it bother her adoptive parents, who shrugged and said, "Oh well."

At age eighteen, Lexi graduated high school and migrated to the gay scene in New York's Greenwitch Village. The gay scene, more so than the straight world, welcomed her.

• • •

Lexi enrolled Max in the grade school just off New York's Sixth Avenue. The school saw him as short, broader than the other kids—and therefore not normal. Max was assigned to a class for the retarded.

• • •

That first day after school. Max was walking home with Denny, who really was retarded, when four second graders, two in front, two in the back, surrounded Denny and Max. One shouted, "Look at the retards," while one of them punched Max in the face.

• • •

Charley, a neighborhood guy, told the cop, "Big mistake. Max punched him back, hit him in the stomach and it looked like the kid had been hit with a wrecking ball. He folded up and was falling face forward when I got my foot under the kid's face quick enough that I could ease it down and keep him from cracking down face-first on the cement."

"What," the cop sad, "about the other kids?"

"They saw and took off running."

Sergeant Swift looked at Max, seeing the resemblance, he said, "You Lexi Brauny's kid?"

"Yeah."

Sergeant Swift looked to Rooky Patrolman Andrews. "This boy's mother is Lexi Brauny. She's the manager and bouncer at that gay bar two blocks from here. Gently suggest to her that her son could use some help."

"Gently?"

"Gently. You see how her boy manhandled an older kid."

• • •

Max's mouth had stopped bleeding by the time Lexi got there. Lexi demanded, "Sergeant, what's going on?"

"Your son was walking Denny home when four second graders decided to beat up on some retards. One of them hit your son and then Max hit him back. A neighbor reported seeing this and said the second grader dropped like a rock."

"My son is not retarded, has never been in a fight before, and he doesn't yet understand how strong he is. Denny lives down the street from us and we'll get him home and then I'm going to take my son back to that school and find out what the hell's going on."

"Lexi, don't do anything could get you arrested, nothing violent."

"I'll think on it, but I make no promises."

• • •

Ms. Goodwin, was moving with quick steps and a harried look when Denny, seeing his mother, rushed forward and into her arms. She then looked to Lexi, who said, "Some older kids thought it might be fun to beat up on two different kinds of kids. My son taught them this had been a bad idea. I don't think they'll want to try that again. I'm taking Max with me when I go down to that school. I have a few things on my mind."

Mrs. Goodwin looked to Lexi and Max, saw the fire burning in Lexi's eyes, and said, "Thank you, and thank you Max."

. . .

Lexi was walking with quick steps, which was usual, when her step stopped. "Max," she said, "When we get to that school don't you say anything unless I ask you to."

Years later, Max would speak of this. "The two of us headed for the office of Vice Principle Cruise and I did like Mom said. Mom sounded almost timid. She said, 'is my son being assigned to a class for the retarded?'"

Max stifled a giggle and thought, *that does not sound like my mom.* Vice Principle Cruise, looking through her records, said, "We prefer the term mentally challenged. He does appear to be challenged."

"My son doesn't say much—couldn't you reassign him?"

"I'm sorry. We couldn't do that."

"Come on son, we're leaving."

Vice Principle Cruise might have felt less smug if she had seen the grin, outside the school, that lit up Lexi's face. She looked at Max and said, "That woman is an idiot, and now she's put her tit in the ringer of a possible lawsuit."

. . .

Attorney Tubman had Max evaluated by three different child psychologists. Looking up from reading their reports, Tubman said, "Lexi, let us hope they stick by their initial decision; God how I hope they allow this to go to Court."

They did.

In Court, Director Gresham had said, "I have a report from teacher Ms. Jacobs stating that when young Max Brauny was shown a picture of two apples and asked to point to the apple that was biggest, he simply stared open-mouthed, and from the second hour on, for the rest of the day, he sat at his desk either asleep or in a stupor. That is not normal. And in a class for the normal that would be a distraction. Just looking at the boy and his mother is enough to tell you that they are not normal."

Judge Siroco was not the handsomest of men. He said, "So, appearance was a determining factor in your decision not to allow this boy a normal education?"

Director Gresham swallowed hard, now realizing she had stepped in it.

Attorney Tubman said, "Your Honor, stigmatizing this boy as below average has been damaging and is unconscionable. I have here three evaluations by three eminent child psychologist, all stating that young Max Brauny's acumen is exceptional for someone his age rather than below average."

"Let me see those reports."

Siroco took his time. Then looking up, he said, "These reports state that Max Brauny has already acquired mathematical and reading skills that measure up to a second grade level and that his mechanical aptitude is quite high for someone six years old. How do I know that the boy they evaluated was really Max Brauny? I take it the young man in the back of this courtroom is Mister Max Brauny?"

"He is Your Honor."

"Mister Brauny, will you step foreward please." Judge Siroco said, "I ask you, why didn't you answer when you were asked which was the big apple and which was the little apple?"

Max frowned. "It was a dumb question. I know the difference between big and little."

Judge Siroco held up a placard. "Can you read this? Max looked and said, "In God we trust."

The Judge nodded and said, "Who taught you how to read?"

"My Mom, plus the kid show on TV."

"Uh huh. Now I'd like to ask you a tough question, a question even grownups might have trouble with."

Max nodded, swallowed, and said, "Okay."

"If a train engine was heading south at forty miles an hour and billowing smoke, while a light wind was blowing eastward, where would the smoke be? Take your time."

"Behind the train."

"Thank you young man. Please retake your seat."

Judge Siroco said, "I have been a Judge in this Court for many a year, and I thought I'd heard everything. That the Educational System, charged with educating our young, would discriminate, deliberately deny this young man the education he deserves based solely on appearance, and attempt to justify this discrimination by labeling this bright young man as mentally challenged, is unconscionable. One might question whether the Department of Education was more interested in stacking a class quota for the mentally challenged than in educating our young. I find this reprehensible."

"Attorney Tubman, do you have anything further to say?"

"I do Your Honor. Since the State of New York's Public School System has refused to provide this young man with the public education he deserves, I believe the State of New York is obligated to provide this young with private tutoring for at least two hours a day during those days others will be receiving a public education in preparation for entering a Public High School. Plus, I will send them my bill."

"Do you have any other requests?"

"We have not Your Honor."

"So be it. It is the ruling of this Court that the State of New York will provide Plaintiff Max Brauny with two hours of private tutoring on each public school day for the period of the next eight years. This case is adjourned."

The gavel came down.

• • •

Years later Max would say, "I was only six years old, when my Mom set me up for private tutoring two hours a day, five days a week, plus homework. Also, mom taught me how to cook and I absorbed my mom's frugality. I hadn't yet learned the word frugality, but that's what it was."

Chapter Two—Friends

Again, Max asked, "Mom, do I have a father? Where is he?"

This time Lexi relented. "I'd been hearing that anything goes in Amsterdam. You and I, our shoulder, elbow, hip and knee joints are broader than what others have while our forearms and lower legs are shorter, compared to our uppers, than what is the norm for the larger society, Our spinal columns are more advanced than what others have, and in France, after I won my Olympic Gold, set all those Women's Weightlifting records, rather than returning home right away, I took a side trip to Amsterdam. I wanted to find out about the anything that goes in Amsterdam. That was when I saw this man . . . and we stared at each other. We had the same heavy bone structure, the same pronounced bone ridge running across our brows, the same reddish hair, hazel eyes and looking at each other was like looking in a mirror, —we started laughing.

"I knew that Neanderthal males had averaged out at a height of 5 feet 7 inches and a weight of about 195 robust pounds, same height and weight as me. Your father was 5 foot 8 and weighed 210—the two of us, probably due to a better diet, were even heavier boned and broader than the now supposedly extinct Neanderthal.

"No one in the world looked like the two of us. "We looked like brother and sister, like twins. We had our DNA checked, we were not related by blood—but we were definitely of the same species."

"Mom, was he from Amsterdam?"

"His passport said that his name was Larry Gutman and that he was from Argentina, while his accent was pure Boston. He said he was in Amsterdam on business. I asked Larry what kind of business and he said, 'That's something we don't talk about.' I didn't ask again."

"Did you love him Momma?"

"With all my heart. He was as strong as me, and the only man I ever loved—ever went to bed with—. We were together for ten days and then we saw this little Asian man. The little man said something in a language I didn't recognize. Larry turned to me, looking serious, shook his head, and handed me a packet from his inside coat pocket.

"He said, 'I have to leave.' I thought, *I'll never see you again,* and I never did.'"

"He's my father?"

"He is. Later, I looked in the packet. Larry had left me $5,000 American."

• • •

When Max got older Lexi took him on runs around the reservoir in Central Park. Lexi devoted more time to her son than she did to any girlfriend—much to the detriment of her love life. "Max," she said, "if you choose, you could be a professional football player or a professional boxer. Marciano was 5'7," weighed in at 189 pounds, and never lost a fight in either the amateurs or the pros."

Max was bouncing a tennis ball off the brownstone wall with his right hand and then spearing the bounce with his left hand.

"When you grow up," Lexi said, "you could, if you wanted, have a career in football, wrestling or boxing."

"Mom, that would be easy and what everyone expects. What they don't expect is that I want to play baseball."

Lexi didn't say anything, not yet anyway.

• • •

One thing Max loved about his Mom was that she always listened. Christmas Day, she took him by subway to the warehouse space she had rented up in Mount Vernon. A pitching machine had been set it up to deliver pitches while nets had been hung to contain what was hit.

Former big league baseball hitting Coach Ron Lyle said, "Your mother," Ron said, "hired me to teach you how to conduct a proper batting practice. You move well, you're built more like a football player, but, if you have the eye for it, if you follow my instructions, work your ass off, and if you ever learn to hit a curveball, then one day you might have a career in baseball."

. . .

So now Max was spending two hours a day five days a week in private tutoring and two hours a day seven days a week pounding the ball in batting practice. It was true enough that Max never did look like a baseball player, didn't look like anything or anyone other than his Mom, but followed Ron's instructions, batting from both the left side of the plate and from the right side, he worked his ass off. The machine had been set up so that the ball usually came in waist high, but when it came in lower he had trouble with it . . . so he reset the machine to send the balls lower and over time he upped the speed. From the beginning, Max was a worker.

In time he would learn to hit the curveball. Springtime his mom signed him up for little league baseball—and he pounded the ball—even those coming in low.

His muscularity raised the question, "is he on steroids?"

When asked, Max said, "My Mom allowed me to be tested for drugs only that one time. After she died, how many drug tests have I taken since then?—I've lost count."

. . .

Max was there when the police knocked on their door. Lexi was notified that her adoptive parents were killed in a home invasion gone bad. Only time Max ever saw tears in his mother's eyes.

Those who inherit from the deceased are automatically suspect. Her parents had been wealthy. Lexi being a different kind of woman, ran a bar owned by mob boss Fat Tony Antonio. Automatically, Lexi was a person of interest. The cops looked for a connection between Fat Tony and the killings. They looked—looked hard, and there was nothing.

Then one of the robbers tried to pawn a wedding band that had Grandfather's name engraved in it. The cops looked for connections between those two idiots and Fat Tony, but again—there was nothing.

Max reported, "My Mom was frugal, an extrovert who enjoyed the company of men, women, gay, straight, you name it, and while she knew and liked them all, it was slender young women who rang Mom's chimes.

"For my Mom," Max said, "the arrival of puberty had been a welcome challenge. For me, with the advent of puberty, I became self-conscious. Miff Trotter was a little older than me and lived down the block. She was cute as hell, her mother was black and her father was white. Whenever I was around Miff, I stammered and my face burned and turned red. Seeing this, my Mom said, "Son, Miff is not for you. She doesn't know it yet, and don't you tell her, but she will be going on the gay scene."

Max thought, *Puberty should be outlawed.*

With a sigh, Lexi said, "The gay scene is more relaxed, more accepting of differences, which is lucky for me, but even so I have difficulty connecting. "Max, I'm sorry to say, the hetero sexual scene is more rigid, less forgiving than the gay scene."

• • •

Gert Connery lived across the street. Her looks were okay, but nothing special. She was a young woman others might not notice until she spoke—but then others would listen— Miff said, "I just love hearing you talk."

Gert turned to her and said, "I know. And I love you too."

Miff's hand covered her mouth. Surprised, embarrassed, yet flattered, she said, "Oh my." It was at that moment that Miff accepted that she was gay and that she wanted Gert. They shared their first kiss at age fifteen. Max was happy for them, but for himself, he was needy, felt all alone.

Gert talked her way into a job at a coffee house down on Mc-Dougall Street and, soon enough, Gert was the one rendering the poetry readings, got a raise, rented her own apartment on West Tenth Street, and Miff moved in with her.

Gert"s father, longshoreman Mick Connery, was a racist and a righteous catholic. He drank too much, was widowed, and was the loneliest of men. After Gert left, for two years, Mick held onto his prejudices as if they were the only thing keeping him afloat. Then, one morning, Mick woke up and said to himself, *I can't do this anymore. I need help.* He turned to Alcoholics Anonymous.

Mick was three months sober when he woke up thinking about the previous evenings AA Meeting. The topic of discussion had been the principle of 'Acceptance is the Key.' Mick said to himself, *what the hell*, and let go of his old ideas. He didn't drown, accepted that he was an alcoholic, accepted that his daughter was a lesbian, and accepted that he liked Miff.

Chapter Three—Alone

On a blustery March day, the Police came knocking on Max's door. From the looks on their faces he knew, right off, that it was bad. He learned that Lexi had been heading into the Subway when someone put a gun to the back of her head and pulled the trigger. Detective Klaus, from the questions he was asking, was searching for a Mob connection to the hit on Lexi. Max shook his head, cut through all that and said, "Betty Bolen. Had to be Betty Bolen."

. . .

Max, seeing his Mom laid out, thought she didn't look too bad, sort of peaceful, kissed her and confirmed the identification."

They picked up Betty Bolen in Penn Station and she still had the gun in her purse. One of the cops said, "Her not pitching the gun saved us and the Courts a lot of trouble. It's a good thing most of these mutts are so stupid."

. . .

Mob boss Fat Tony Antonio arranged for Lexi's Memorial Service. Mobsters, guys from the world of competitive weight lifting, men, women, some gay, some straight, showed up and there were tears. Max was grateful at seeing Miff and Gert show up.

After the Memorial Service Max took his Mom's ashes by subway to Coney Island. The tide appeared to be either halfway in or halfway out and he walked out into the water until it reached up to his chest. The tide was going out so he said, "Goodby Mom," and let her ashes go out with the tide.

• • •

Max was Subpoenaed to appear at Betty Bolen's trial as a witness for the Defense. Max said, "I'm willing to testify."

The Head Prosecutor, wide eyed, shook his head and said, "No. You don't want to do that."

"Why?"

"Max, if you take the stand, the Defense will twist everything you say to make your mother look bad. They'll use everything you say to justify Betty Bolen having taken your mother's life."

"Show me."

Prosecutor Higgins sighed and said, "This is what will happen if you take the stand." He came at Max, looking all friendly and sympathetic, only to switch and try every dirty trick in the book. It didn't work.

Higgins was surprised and said, "Max, how'd you get so smart?"

"Watching Mom. Both of us get stares and shitty remarks. So many times I've seen Mom not get defensive, turn the tables, and put the other on the defensive—Mom always said, 'turn it, that's the key'—Mom and I never defend—we turn it and put it back on them.'"

The Prosecution Team paused—looked at each other. Then Prosecutor Higgins said, "We could catch them by surprise if we let him testify."

• • •

When Court reconvened, Defense Attorney Andrew Brasse arose and said, "The Defense now calls Mr. Max Brauny to the stand." The Judge looked to the prosecution table and said, "Does the Prosecution have any objection to this witness?" They entered into a brief huddle. When they broke, the lead prosecutor said, "Not at this time your Honor."

Attorney Brasse, rubbing his hands together and sounding all friendly, said, "So, may I call you Max?"

"Yes Sir."

"You lived with your mother didn't you?"

"Yes Sir."

"And she brought different women home with her didn't she?"

"Yes Sir."

So . . . by her example, she taught you that it's okay to bed as many women as you possibly can, bed them and then dump them."

"Is that what you think?"

"That is what we are attempting to establish here." His voice rose. "Again, I ask you, did Lexi Brauny, by her example, teach you that it's okay to bed as many women as you can, bed them, and then dump them?"

"By her example, she taught me never to lie to them."

The defense attorney turned to the bench. "Your Honor, I motion that this is a hostile witness and that his testimony be stricken from the record."

The Judge said, "You opened the door counselor. Motion denied." She then looked to Max and said, "Mr. Brauny, you may continue."

"My mother always said, "For God's sake find a decent girl who will commit to you and you commit to her and don't ever waver or you will end up like me spending the rest of your days looking over your shoulder!"

Betty Bolen's pistol had fired the bullet in another, a non-fatal shooting, and she received a sentence of life without parole.

Max doubled his time on the pitching machine.

• • •

A voice on the phone said, "This is Doctor Stacy Gladwell. Am I speaking with Max Brauny?"

"Yup. That's me."

"This is awkward. We had been corresponding with your mother and we had hoped to have the two of you, as our guests, here in Seattle at the University of Washington . . . .. Who is your legal guardian?"

"Me—there's only me. Mom's parents are dead. Social Service

looks in on me from time to time, I pay my rent, my insurance, my bills, my Mom taught me how to shop and cook, After the monthly bills are paid, I take out no more than fifty a week for groceries and walking around money— didn't last week because I still had over fifty in my pocket. West Tenth is pretty much free of drugs, and the local cops and Fat Tony keep an eye on who comes around me. Everyone's satisfied I'm functioning OK."

"We had intended to invite you and your mother here for a series of tests. Would you consider coming to Seattle? We'd pick up the expense for your transportation and for the time you're here. Perhaps we can learn from each other."

Max didn't hesitate. He said, "Send me a ticket. Greyhound. I've never been out of New York State, not even across the Hudson to New Jersey, and I'd like to see some of the country—Right now I could use a change of scenery."

Max was 15 years old, didn't have a parent, didn't have a girl-friend, and it was tearing him up.

• • •

Outside of baseball, Max had few loves. One of his loves was the language of Shakespeare; it flowed. Even as a boy he could recite from memory many of Hamlet's soliloquies. It occurred to him that, *if a girl were to come on the bus and see me engrossed in reading a classic, maybe, just maybe, she'd risk sitting with me.* He bought a paperback edition of Hamlet.

Coming out of Sioux Falls there were only two empty seats left. One was across the aisle and the other was next to Max. One girl and a fulsome Catholic nun came aboard. The girl was maybe fourteen-fifteen. Walking down the aisle, seeing Max apparently engrossed in a book, she slid into the empty seat.

Wow! Max thought, it worked . . . now what?

Max scrunched myself up as hard as he could against the window and hid in his book.

The empty seat across from them was taken up by Catholic Nun Sister Mary Beth. Max's ploy with the book had worked, and the girl was maybe five foot, light brown hair, nice face, had a cute bod, and she smelled nice. But now what? . . . After maybe an hour, and still not having spoken, Max closed his book, stared out the window, and drifted off in fantasies of emergencies rising up and his coming to the rescue of the fair maid now sitting beside him.

He thought, *This is crazy, she's sitting right beside me and I don't have a clue on what to do next.* Again, he took up the book. Sister Mary Beth caught Max's eye and nodded. He thought, *I think she's someone who sees and understands everything— better than I do anyway.*

• • •

The girl was named Josie Gilmore. She said, "What are you reading?" and he showed her the book.

In a singsong voice she said, "Shakespeare! I thought you'd be reading about wrestling or football or something."

Later, Max would say, "my fantasy's crumbled . . . and my pecker shriveled. Just more of the same old shit.

"And why," he said, "would you think that?"

She withered and he reopened his book. After a time she said, "I'm sorry, really, really sorry." From across the aisle, Sister Mary Beth heard and raised her eyes up to the ceiling while Max relented and hope was revived.

He said, "It's okay. . . I'm oversensitive. I get this all the time. Football, pushing other kids around, hurting them and making them cry— I'm not interested in that. In baseball I get to cut loose, smack the ball as hard as I can. I like that."

Her nodding and attempting to put a smile on the situation thawed him out. He said, "I was the third baseman on the American Little League Team. In Taiwan it was me hit the homerun that won us the Little League World Championship—To hit that home run—what a grand feeling that was!"

The ice, he hoped, was broken. But embarrassed, Max said, "I'm going to close my eyes for a moment."

He awoke to find the girl asleep leaning into him . . . it was the nicest feeling he had ever known. Sister Mary Beth was awake. She gave him a cautionary look that he didn't understand.

• • •

Max said, "Where you headed Josie?"

"Dufer. It's my home, just outside Seattle. What about you?"

"University of Washington. The doctors there want to figure out why I'm so broad, or why you're all so skinny. Then I'll probably go back to New York. You have a high school in Dufer?"

Josie nodded.

"They have a baseball team?"

"They do . . . they never won a game last year."

"I could change that."

Josie had her cue, but she ignored it, said nothing.

"Losing my Mom knocked me for a loop and I didn't start High school. Now I have to."

Josie exhibited no sign of curiosity and there was no suggestion from Josie that Max could go to High School in Dufer.

On their last morning on the bus Josie said, "My sister's dating the Captain of the football team . . . the boys at our school are awful cute—not like you."

There had been hints, but this parting shot said it all. Josie was one mean chick.

• • •

Chapter Four—On to Dufur

Bank Manager David Burnside opened Seattle's Wallingford Branch Office promptly at 9AM. Max was the day's first customer and an anomaly, only 16 years old and standing only 5 feet 5 inches tall while being almost as wide and solid as a brick outhouse.

"What can I do for you sir?"

The odd-looking but well-dressed New York Accent said, "I'm relocating so I need a local bank for my checking account."

"Certainly sir. How much do you wish to deposit?"

"Let's start with $20,000.

Seeing check number 101, Bank Manager Burnside didn't even blink when he pushed the silent alarm button—the local Police Station was at the end of the block—Burnside distracted with a patter about the check colors and patterns that were available.

Max made his choices and provided the Motel address to where the checks should be mailed. Exiting, he was confronted by a male/female police team. Detective Gunther Wolff was in plainclothes, badged him, and said, "Turn around and put your hands against the wall." As Max was turning Gunther Wolff tried to spin him— he didn't spin—The 6 foot Detective found himself sitting on the sidewalk. The uniformed officer shocked Max. He shuddered. She shocked him a second time and that staggered him. She shocked him a third time and this time he went down.

• • •

He remembered being in handcuffs and being read his Rights. After being booked, Detective Wolff said, "Here's what we think. You opened up a checking account in New York City for probably $200, traveled cross country to Seattle, and used check number 101 in an attempt to set up a $20,000 line of credit. About as dumb and grandiose a scam as I ever heard. What do you have to say to that?"

Max, not feeling very good, shook his head.

"Nothing to say? Well my, my, my."

On cue, a uniform entered Interrogation and said, "Wolff, the check was good."

Detective Gunther Wolff's face went white and he removed the cuffs. Max was not well, tried to stand, and felt himself falling. Way off . . . Max heard someone say, "Oh shit!"

Max came to in the University Hospital Emergency room, was on a respirator, and had IV's in his arms.

The MD, a medium sized guy wearing scrubs, glasses, and a relieved expression, said, "Do you remember what happened?"

"I opened up a new checking account. When I came out of the bank a guy in plainclothes badged me and then started roughing me up. I pushed him away and the lady in uniform hit me three times with a shocker. I remember being in the Police Station. Then I woke up here."

The Doctor's Jaw set. "They shocked you twice and you didn't go down so they shocked you close to your heart the third time. The evidence to that is clearly marked on your chest. They're not supposed to do that. I'm having you placed in the Intensive Care Unit."

• • •

Max was accompanied by an attorney when he went to collect his belongings from the Wallingford Station's front desk. He counted his money and said, "There's only $247 here. You've shorted me $100. I made a substantial bank deposit and for this I was assaulted by the Police, tazored, booked, hospitalized, and robbed. You better come up with my $100."

They did.

• • •

Max was living in a dorm at the University of Washington, sometimes referred to as the U Dub. He was under observation 24/7 and they put him through every physical, mental, psychological, medical, stress-test imaginable, even sleep-deprivation tests.

Some of the tests they dreamed up were truly exotic.

Doctor Gladwell said, "We assumed, from the skeletal remains of Neanderthals, their heavy bone structure, that they possessed super-human strength. You've pretty-well nailed down that supposition. Your forearms and lower legs, in comparison to those of modern man, are proportionally shorter in relationship to your upper limbs. This gives you more leverage for power movements but lessens your hand and foot speed, yet you still have decent hand and foot speed. So far we've learned your mathematical and mechanical aptitudes are high while your ability to abstract is quite high. Your vision is exceptional while your hearing is low average. The day may come when you will need hearing aids. The contradiction to this is that your primary cognitive mode of relating is focused more on what you hear rather than on what you see."

"One of the surprises that awaited us is your love of language and the ease of your having committed Hamlet's soliloquies to memory.

Doctor Gladwell continued, "There are two areas where you're vulnerable. You have a low heat tolerance and heat exhaustion could be a factor in your life. There is also the high caloric intake you require. The extinction of large mammals as a source of caloric intake, plus interbreeding with homo sapiens, may have led to the demise of the Neanderthal as a separate species, I say may . . . we can at present only speculate about why the Neanderthal went extinct.

"Initially, we were concerned that there might be some imbalance in your hormonal system, but so far we've found nothing to suggest a need for medical intervention. Our calculations indicate that you should reach physical maturity at about five foot seven inches and around 200 plus pounds."

"What if I have children Doc? Will they be like me or will they be like their mother?"

"We don't have the answer to that but you're quite capable of having children. What we do know is that 1.5% to 4% of non-

African, modern human DNA comes from Neanderthals while thirty-five percent of your own DNA comes from the Neanderthal. What mixture of your DNA with the mother's DNA would be present in the child is something we can't predict."

Twenty days of this and Max said, "I've had enough. Finish it."

Josie had ignored him when Max said he could turn things around for the Dufer baseball team. That had pissed him off and he took a cab to Dufer, had the cabbie drive him around the town, located the High school, saw that Dufer, outside of the usual franchise establishments, had only two local businesses, a roof truss factory and a large greenhouse. "Okay," he said, "let me off at McDonald's."

Entering McDonald's, as luck would have it, Josie Gilmore was there, seated with her back to the door, and was regaling others at her table with the tale of the weird looking kid she had to sit next to on the bus. Johnny Reddish, everyone called him Johnny Red, looked up, saw Max, and immediately knew Max was the kid Josie was talking about. His eyes went wide and he stared. Josie swiveled about, her eyes registered on Max, then wheeled back facing in the previous direction.

Wide heels from his custom-made shoes clicking on the floor, Max walked around the silent table until he was facing Josie. She arose and headed for the door. Johnny Red said, "Yeah, she does things like that. Take a seat Max."

• • •

Rental Agent Willis took Max on a tour of available rental properties. The one just off Dell Road suited Max. The cabin was stuck back in the woods about 40 yards. The quiet was different from New York. That night he heard an owl hoo hooing—at least he thought it must be an owl, but otherwise, all that quiet was weird.

• • •

Max flew back to New York, picked up his mother's car, bought a trailer and loaded up his pitching machine, the backdrop nets, and his Mom's barbell. He had been through Driving School, had a driver's license, but had never driven on the freeway. Taking off for US Highway 80, he drove well below the speed limit for the first thousand miles, sweated blood, but by the time he reached Montana, he had grown comfortable with freeway driving.

• • •

Dufer High accepted Max as a Freshman.

That first high school day, Max was sitting at a cafeteria empty table and with his back to the wall when Eddy Cottrel left his table and with two teammates following, he sat down across from Max. "Shorty," he said, "you look strong enough, you turning out for football?"

"No. I'll be turning out for baseball."

"Ah yes. The wimps game. Shorty, you're weird-looking and you have a funny accent. Josie belongs to me, so you don't get to talk to her. These are the rules and you will obey them or I will hurt you. I've got the speed, the reach, the punch. You understand?"

"You better learn my name, otherwise I'll have to kick your ass."

Eddie sighed, "I think we need to go out behind the gym and come to an understanding."

"Agreed."

They trooped out and others followed.

Behind the gym Eddie turned to Max and said, "I'm sorry about this but you need to know." Eddie had fast hands but so did Max. His Mom had bought boxing gloves and they boxed. Lexi had kept her punches light but insisted he punch full power, only not to hit her on the boobs.

Eddie feinted with a left and threw his right. Max brushed Eddie's incoming punch aside and hit him in the chops. Eddie staggered— was out on his feet—Max gave him a light push, Eddie landed on his butt, and then Max headed back to his table.

He was still working on lunch when Eddie returned. Everyone was watching. Eddie swallowed, walked up to Max's table and asked, "What's your name?"

"Max Brauny."

"Pleased to meet you Max. Are you sure you wouldn't like to turn out for football?"

• • •

Max received a visit from Coach Rodgers who said, "You have legs like tree trunks and a huge chest. We could use you on the football team."

• • •

Max didn't turn out for football, but he did attend the team's first game and Johnny Red, the kid who had welcomed Max at McDonald's, was the quarterback. Johnny was being pounded into the turf every other play, had no time to pass or even hand off before defenders were pounding on him.

Dufer lost twenty-four to nothing.

• • •

Max walked into the gloom of that locker room and said, "Coach, you put me in next week and I'll knock some of those guys on their asses." Heads, even Johnny Red's, lifted. Eddie Cottrell said, "It's about time you got here. We could use some help." Coach Rodgers cheered up.

• • •

In his first game, they put Max on the other team's best defensive player, their team's right defensive tackle. He was a Junior, Max was a freshman, but Max didn't let him across the line of scrimmage, and put him on his butt more than once. Dufer lost 17 to 14, but they hadn't embarrassed themselves. For the team's third game they played Max at center. On running plays, Max would center the ball, get an arm under each of the lineman in front of him and march those two back into the secondary. Johnny Red had a great passing arm and if you gave him time in the pocket, he'd tear you up. But definitely, when Johnny Red was flushed out of the pocket, he was not what someone would refer to as being sweet on his feet.

• • •

At the U Dub, Max said, "It's crazy. One minute I was this weird guy, the next minute I was a hero. If anyone can explain to me how high school works I sure would like to hear it."

"Social scientists," Doctor Allan Burkin said, "waste a lot of time in a futile search for the dynamic event that leads to social change. It's a ridiculous waste of time and money.

"We like to flatter ourselves with the belief that we are a rugged individualistic species, and are therefore moved only by cataclysmic forces. This false belief drives us to not accept the simple reality that we are a herd species. One can only imagine what it would be like on the freeway if everyone was a rugged individualist and each of us was doing his own thing. Epidemic and sudden changes in clothing fashions, the music we listen to, religious beliefs, the popularity of cults, hushpuppy shoes, you name it, are not triggered by momentous, measurable events or forces. They begin with a single movement or thought that, since we are a herd species, what appeals to the one then spreads by contagion."

Doctor Gladwell said, "Eddie Cottrell was the first turned to you and the rest of the herd followed, "That answer your question?"

"Why isn't it recognized if it's that simple?"

"We like to think of ourselves as rugged individuals, not sheep.

• • •

Odd-looking Max, by putting on football pads, had suddenly turned into a beauty. Dufer lost only three games Max's Freshman year. After their last football game he said, "Johnny Red, I've got a pitching machine at my house. Want to see it?"

"No shit? You've got a pitching machine? Hell yes I want to see it!"

Johnny Red was the best hitter on Dufer's baseball team. Max said, "In Little League play I was started out as a catcher, but on hot days, wearing all that equipment, the heat was so bad that I would damn near pass out, plus, my arm wasn't good enough for a catcher or to play outfield, I was too short for first base, and I was shifted to third base.

Johnny Red loved baseball, had that slingshot for an arm that a catcher needs, and as a Freshman, Johnny had hit for a 260 BA. Every chance he had, Johnny Red was in the batting cage at Max's house. As a catcher, balls in the dirt had sometimes got past Johnny Red so when Johnny and Max completed their turns in the batter's box, they reset the pitching machine to deliver pitches in the dirt in front of home plate. All through basketball season bad bounces had banged into Johnny, left him with purple bruises, but he didn't quit. By the time baseball season came around, nothing was getting past Johnny Red.

Every night, except for those nights when the weather was bad, Johnny Red and Max pounded out balls from the pitching machine.

When baseball season opened Max was all attitude and pounding the ball for a 400 plus BA. Johnny Red upped his batting average to 310, hit the low ball well, and if they left it up in the zone Johnny Red killed it.

Definitely, Johnny Red and Max had upped the interest in their baseball team.

Johnny Red said, "You're better built for football."

"Yeah. But it's not what I want. Baseball is what I want."

Chapter Five—The FBI

Max arrived home and found he was not alone. The man sitting in his house was a Lexi/Max look-alike. All three of them were heavy boned, muscular, had red hair, pale skin and hazel eyes. Dazed, Max said, "You my father?"

"I am. I was in Taiwan while they were checking you out for drugs."

"Same thing happens here in the States. They check my blood, analyze hair samples, skin plugs, urine samples . . . they throw the works at me. I gave up counting the number of drug tests."

His father nodded. "I saw you hit that homerun against the Chinese team. I wasn't in the stands, I was some distance back, but I saw it!"

"When I rounded third I thought I saw a red-haired broad guy standing back from all those skinny Chinese. But when I looked again, there was no one there. I asked myself if what I had seen was real. You didn't hang around. Why?"

"If I'd stayed, Interpol would have been all over me, all over you."

"You know Mom died?"

"I know. I met your Mom in Amsterdam, loved her, but couldn't stay. Always, when I'm abroad, I had to keep moving. This is both my hello and my goodbye to my son.

"I've deposited a quarter million in your account so the Feds are going to pay you a visit. You can't tell them anything they don't already know so tell the truth. They'll give you a hard time if you lie or hold back."

Max had been about to say something when he heard a car horn. His father said, "That's for me. When the cops show up, and they will, don't lie. Tell them everything."

He had dropped in for a minute and then he was gone. Max thought, *Jesus. He's my father and I don't feel anything.* Then he began wailing, sobbing. By the time he got a hold on himself, his throat was aching. He asked himself, *Jesus, what was that all about?*

• • •

Two uptight FBI Agents, lean, in single-breasted suits and dark shades, did show up—dramatically. They pulled Max out of class, transported him to Seattle's Federal Building, and a large black man, expensively dressed, followed by the two less-impressive-looking white guys, entered the Interrogation Room. The black guy introduced himself as Inspector Roderious. The Inspector said, "Think about telling the truth. Failure to cooperate will lead to serious consequences. Do you understand?"

"Hell no!"

Roderious blinked, and then, to almost every question he asked, Max answered, "I don't know."

One question was, "How often do you see your father?"

"Only seen him twice. Once last week and once I saw him behind third base at the Little League game we played in Taiwan. We never spoke that first time and then he was gone."

"If you'd never seen him before and you had never spoken with him, how did you know he was your father?"

Max thought, *what an asshole,* even though he didn't say it. What he did say was, "Look at me. Is there anyone else in the world that looks like me or my father?"

He took a cab back to Dufer. When fellow students asked what that had been about, he put his thumb and first finger together and run them across his lips as if zippering them. This intimidated even the school staff . . . sometimes intimidation is transformed into acceptance, or something that at least looks like acceptance; Max thought, *it's better than nothing.*

. . .

Dufer Police Chief Willard Ash paid Max a visit. Even though this was the Northwest, Willard looked like a caricature of what was sometimes portrayed on TV as a good-old-boy and mildly-sadistic Southern Sheriff.

Chief Willard said, "Detective Gunther Wolff, paid me a visit. He said I needed to keep an eye on you, so I'll be watching you boy!"

It was rumored that Max had millions but that was not true . . . not quite. Even with what he had received from his father and his inheritance from his mother he had less than a million. How that rumor got started wasn't clear, but the word was out that Max had money, a hideaway house in the woods, and was a decent baseball and football player.

Josi came stalking. She impressed on Max how badly she needed a car. When that didn't fly she said, "I would really, really like a nice engagement ring."

"I'm sure you would." Then Max turned his back on her and walked away.

Josie didn't look exactly heartbroken—more like pissed.

. . .

Meanwhile, Max was still being tested at the U Dub. "What's the verdict Doc? How do I stack up?"

"You stack up at five feet six inches tall, weigh 185 pounds, the same height and possibly heavier than an adult male Neanderthal, plus the bone density of your sixteen- year old body is as robust, more so actually, than that of an adult Neanderthal. You're sixteen years old, and unlike the Neanderthal, we know from studying their bone and teeth, that they experienced frequent famine, you've never missed a meal in your life and you're still growing. You have a bull neck, your hand-eye coordination is as good if not better than anyone we've so far tested, and your facial structure clearly indicates the influence of Neanderthal genes.

"Because of modern man's imperfect transition to upright

walking from our nearest relatives, knuckle-walking primates, our spinal columns, when assuming upright locomotion, were forced into piecemeal adaptations, and that is why modern man is subject to so much back pain. Your spinal column, as was that of the Neanderthal, is more advanced than that of our modern man, and the physical power you possess is intimidating."

• • •

When Max returned home after baseball practice, he'd fix a meal, mostly boiled vegetables, chicken or steak, salads, and sometimes salmon. Johnny Red would show up and they'd go into the batting cage. Private schooling had left Max well-prepared academically for High School and homework didn't take long. Weekends, along with batting practice, Max did squats, bench presses, and then switched to the two Olympic lifts which were quick lifts requiring balance and speed.

• • •

The winds of change at Dufer High ebbed and flowed. That first day in Dufer High started with people leery, watching Max and waiting for something to happen. Then he became a football hero, and the winds of acceptance swirled even more with the finding that his father was a wanted International Criminal. The spotlight was also shining on the fact that Max live alone and had money.

• • •

Straight out, Johnny Red said, "Max, if you have children, will they be like you or like their mother?"

"Tough question. If the mother retained any Neanderthal DNA, they could be like me. Otherwise, I'm pretty sure they'd be more like their mother—I hope they'd be like their mother."

Johnny said, "How'd you come to be like you?"

"Johnny, don't you ever talk about this. We don't know all the story, but what we do know is that modern humans, Homo Sapiens, evolved prior to the ice age known as Marine Isotope Stage 6, that was between 195,000 and 123,000 years ago. The planet was locked in a cold, arid ice age and that event triggered a dying off of Homo Sapiens."

"How you know this."

"Doctor Gladwell. The southern coast of Africa would have been the one area where modern humans could have survived during that time. The area harbored an abundance of shellfish and was the only place in the world having a class of plants called fynbos that had bulbs below the ground that were rich in stored carbohydrates."

"Uh huh. Energy food. Keeps you going."

"At the close of the Stage 6 Ice Age, this small number of modern humans multiplied, spread outward and filled up the African continent. Little is known about the evolution of the Neanderthal, or why we disappeared. The species of hominids known as Homo Erectus traveled out of Africa and may have evolved into Neanderthals. Some in the field suspect that Neanderthals evolved out of Homo Heidelbergensis."

"So what happened to the Neanderthals?"

"About 50,000 years ago, Homo Sapiens, modern man, migrated out of Africa and entered the colder lands of the Neanderthals. The domain of the Neanderthal was vast, yet the population was spread out and probably never exceeded more than 15,000 individuals. Encounters between Neanderthals and Homo Sapiens would have been rare, but us hominids being a sexy group, interbreeding would have happened. I am the living proof that this interbreeding occurred. Still, 15,000 years after the first encounters between modern man and the Neanderthal, the Neanderthals were gone. My father and I are all that's left."

"So you're as big as the Neanderthal?"

"Bigger. It's clear that both my parents carried Neanderthal DNA and passed it on to me. Of the thousands of combinations of letters in our DNA, why some got turned on and others turned off we don't know. My Neanderthal DNA was turned on, and, unlike the Neanderthal, I've never missed a meal, so I'm heavier, wider, even taller than the original Neanderthal. Don't you repeat any of this this Johnny."

Chapter Six—Pro Baseball

Johnny Red was a Senior and Max was a Junior when Max signed a huge baseball contract. Johnny Red also signed for a lesser bonus. The two of them then joined the Instructional League in Florida.

They were up early and practiced every day and all day, and then played a complete game. Their high school coach had warned them about the pressure. The heat took everything Max had. Noontime Max would stand for fifteen minutes under a cooling shower.

Johnny Red liked catching, liked feeling in charge, and being a catcher is the fastest route up to The Show.

There was no air conditioning in the Clubhouse, which was old, dingy, dark and without ceiling fans. The Instructional League closed on November fifteen.

Johnny and Max were assigned, from March to October, to the One A Club in Everett, Washington. "Johnny Red," Max said, "I thought I knew all about you. In High School you were quiet. Most of the time you're still quiet, but when you get behind the plate, you always talk. How come?"

"Not always. In High School I called the game, hit, played my position, and that was it, period. As a professional I want more, I want to get inside the batter's head, get him thinking, get him out of his groove. This is a business. I'll talk to the batter about any change in his stance, anything different I notice. Sometimes I make up something. Any way I can, any advantage I can find, I go for it."

Max worked hard, but no harder than Johnny. Baseball Manager Leo Durocher once said, "Nice guys finish last." One thing they learned is that insurance companies liked to hire ex-ballplayers to sell insurance because, if they'd made it as far as Triple A, they'd already developed a competitive edge and the will to win. The prevailing attitude in pro baseball is: It isn't cheating if you don't get caught.

Max said, "I would not have recommended life in the minor leagues to anyone."

On Johnny Red's first appearance in Triple A, Larry Villant was pitching. Villant had been up to The Show, was recovering from elbow surgery, and wanted to put Johnny Red in his place. Twice he shook off Johnny's call. His third call was for a slider. This time Villant nodded yes.

Johnny said, "Watch for a slider." The leadoff batter let the slider go by. Villant shook off the next call. Johnny then called for a fastball and this Villant accepted. Johnny said, "Watch for a fastball. The batter rode the fastball off the left field fence for a solid two base hit. Villant shook off the next call. When he accepted the second call, Johnny told the batter what was coming. He rode it off the Right Field fence for a double. One run was in, a runner on second, and nobody out. Manager Capp came out of the dugout. "Allright!" he growled. "What's going on?"

"Geeze Capp," Johnny Red said, "I don't know . . . He keeps shaking me off and then he gets pounded."

Capp said, "How's his stuff?"

"His stuff's good."

Capp knew what Johnny Red had done, and despite how gruff he sounded, he had a gleam in his eye. "Get it together you two."

When Capp headed back to the dugout Johnny said, "Villant, you stop fucking with me and I'll help you win this game." Everett won the game five to three. Johnny Red had a single and a double. Two hits in five at-bats was damn good for his first game in Triple A.

Capp said, "Lenny Blackburn has the best arm on the team, but he always seems to have one bad inning."

Nothing is casual in baseball. Capp was into seeing how, as a catcher, Johnny Red would deal with this. He didn't have long to wait. Johnny had enough by the second time he caught Lenny. This time, when the problem came up again, Johnny Red marched out to the mound and blew up. "Lenny, you have one strike and three balls. Every time you get behind in the count you run out of guts. You look up at the sky, say a prayer that goes, *It's in your hands now God.* Meanwhile, the batter is also praying, that rather than continue to trim the edges, you'll throw a fastball down the middle and God answers his prayers—because why would God help a gutless wonder like you!"

Mortified and hating Johnny Red's guts, Lenny moved the ball around and got out of the jam. He allowed only three earned runs.

After the game Capp called the front office he said, "This Johnny Red kid's Big League."

Surprise, Max knew that all along.

• • •

The serial killer known as ''The Slasher' struck again. Rosie De-Groot, one of the Baseball Annies, one of those girls who just loved baseball players, had been mutilated and murdered.

Detective Gunther Wolff came nosing around and asking other players what they knew about Max and Rosie. Then he approached Max. "We know you were acquainted with Rosie so why don't you come down to the station and answer a few questions."

Detective Wolff did not directly accuse, but the way he looked at Max was accusing enough. Wolff was becoming a real nuisance.

Chapter Seven—Meet Addie Forester

This is the thing about professional baseball. Even the married with children, when on the road, after the game, all must head for the bar. Max was a ballplayer and never alone except in bed. And there, he was much alone.

• • •

Max came out of the Safeway with a gallon of orange juice. Two women, one black and one white, were sitting at the bus stop. The black woman was slender, attractive, and holding the other woman spell-bound. As Max drew near the black woman looked up, nodded in approval and said, "Beautifully tailored shirt, quality fabric, light blue color, and a Nehru collar. I admire your tailor." Max was seventeen years old. She appeared to be a well-cared for thirty plus, had bypassed any comment about his unique body or facial structure, and instead, she recognized his tailoring. That had never happened before. He said, "Could I drive you somewhere?"

"I'd like that. I'm Addy Forester." Following her directions, they headed for Puyallup. He said, "You got in my car. I'm surprised you'd do that not knowing me."

"No hair stood up on my arms or the back of my neck. So yes, I trust you. I'm staying in the house I inherited from my grandmother and, at the moment, I'm involved in a sticky divorce so I can't invite you into my home right now, but maybe someday."

The house where he delivered Addy was a run down one story building and the yard was a jungle and not at all like the well-kept lady herself. "What I can do," she said, "is give you my phone number."

• • •

The phone number she gave Max didn't work. A week later, he saw Addie at the same bus stop. "That number you gave me doesn't work."

"That can't be. I get calls from Washington DC every week on that phone. "I'll have to check my phone bill. I'm an attorney and I have to get to a business meeting at the Smith Tower in Seattle. My father gave me a Mercedes on my Graduation, but my husband has a set of the keys so I've put my car in storage where he can't find it."

Max was spending a good deal of what little free time he had driving Addie around. "Damn," he reported, "she was entertaining. Once, when we were in a coffee shop, a man walked in the front door, and sort of framed the scene with his two hands as if the scene pleased him."

Addie said, "The new owner just walked in the door."

"The new owner," Max reported, "overheard this, and took a seat at our table and the two of them became engrossed in a lively conversation. People loved talking to Addie. Never in my life have I seen anyone that could match Addie when it came to charming people. The owner told Addie the name of the gated community where he and his wife lived."

"Oh," Addie said, "well then, you probably know my friends Frank and Edna Praaste."

"I saw," Max said, "the owners face change. Her mention of Frank and Edna Praaste made a connection he didn't like and without a word he left the table. It didn't seem to bother Addie—and that made me uneasy."

• • •

"Addie, it seems like every time we drive this last two mile stretch to your house, we see this same messed-up looking guy walking along this same stretch of road."

Looking alarmed, she said, "Don't stop for him. He's tetched."

Max thought, *what college grad refers to someone as tetched?* He told himself that Addie probably had to cover up a humble beginning. He wanted to believe Addie, since she was the most charming companion he had ever met, and second, whenever they entered any new environment, she would lead in radiating confidence and charm. Immediately, those present assumed she was *somebody*. This allowed Max to take a back seat. He wanted to believe, but damn, he had a lot of money to protect and for sure Addie was finding interesting ways into his pocket.

So he hired a private detective.

• • •

Addie announced she had an appetite for Chinese—and off they went. Addie exchanged a few words with the waitress in Chinese.

Max said, "You speak Chinese?"

"Some. I was in China on business for six months last year. Those I did business with spoke English but I picked up some of the language. That brings up something—I have to fly to San Francisco tonight—finalize the business deals I set up in China and finalize my divorce. That should take about three days. When I get back, I think it's time we sat down and decide where we're heading in this relationship."

• • •

Three days later he received a call. "Max," Addie said, "I'm exhausted. It took all my fluid assets to buy off my ex-husband. Thank God, now I'm a free woman. You need to send me $10,000 and we'll straighten out our finances when I get back."

"Addie, you've never been married, you're not an attorney, you never went to college, your real name is Kimberly Shelton, and you're currently on parole. You said you needed to get to the Smith Tower on business but what you needed was to report to your Parole Officer."

"You're a rotten bastard Max! You've been spying on me. This is unforgivable, you playing me and wasting my time!"

"Actually, even with my knowing you being a fraud, not an attorney, you being the funniest and most charming woman I ever met, I thought maybe, just maybe, my having all this money, there might be a chance to work something out. That was before I learned you were playing two others besides me. I learned about the tantrum you threw when Otto had to show three pieces of ID to cash a check and give you the money."

"Those impersonations you run— when you get caught you trot out your history of psychiatric hospitalizations, get transferred to a mental hospital, and when they realize you're not crazy, the hospital discharges you. Addie, in the words of William Shakespeare: Let us become better strangers."

Josie Gilmore had lightened Max's pocketbook somewhat, not enough to hurt, but his ego had been blistered by Kimberly Shelton, AKA Addie Forester.

Chapter Eight—Performance enhancing drugs

Johnny Red and Max made the move to the Mariners together. Catcher Eddy Dickens said, "Johnny Red, you're the team's catcher of the future. My career is winding down but for now I'll be the lead catcher. They're going to play me this year so they can shop me around off-season. As the backup catcher you'll get playing time— enough to show what you're made of."

• • •

Rabbit Warren was the handsomest black man Max had ever seen. He couldn't hit worth a damn, but being the best utility fielder in baseball, able to play any of the infield or outfield positions, draw a walk and steal a base. Rabbit was in his fourteenth year playing Big League Baseball.

Max saw a small-boned young woman sitting with Rabbit. She was two shades lighter than Rabbit, had a delicate and gorgeous face, beautiful eyes, a taut and terrific body, and glistening wavy black hair. When Rabbit left the table Max collared him and said, "That girl sitting with you, she's young enough to be your daughter, who is she?"

"As a matter-of-fact she's my sixteen year old daughter."

Max ducked his head and moved away.

• • •

Rabbit was assigned to coach Max on the finer points of playing third base. His teammates, some of them anyway, were batting 400 plus with the ladies. Rabbit Warren got his nickname, as he hopped from bed to bed, and Rabbit was batting close to a thousand.

Rabbit Warren said, "Max, "other teams seeing you playing third, you being short and blocky, they'll try bunting on you."

"God I hope so. Despite my build I'm sweet on my feet and get to the ball in a hurry. My throw to first is not great, but it's accurate."

"You listen to me and you'll start sooner and get there even quicker."

Max did listen, started sooner, and did get their quicker.

• • •

His now having graduated from the minor leagues, having become a major-league ballplayer—Max also became better looking. Lexi had cautioned her son, "Find a girl who will be true to you, and you be true to her. Play the field like me and you will end up like me, always looking over your shoulder."

Baseball Annies, the girls who 'just love' baseball players, were always there. Max sometimes hooked up with a Baseball Annie. For a shorter or longer period, it was better than nothing, and without them, there really was nothing. He yearned for a committed relationship.

• • •

Max was periodically tested for drugs and he suspected someone, someday, would try to scam him into revealing his formula for the drugs they thought he must be using. Sick of being asked about drugs, He wrote out a formula, carried it in his wallet and memorized it.

Max was hitting the ball well, and agreed to be interviewed on the Allie Machen Show, but on the condition that Allie would not bring up the topic of drugs or drug supplements.

Allie did his warmup monolog, it went well, and the studio audience was polite and attentive. Then Allie brought Max out. They took seats in front of the camera and Allie asked informed questions about the season, but Allie's eyes had a glitter in them and that signaled something was not right. Max thought, *I'll be damned. The guy is loaded.*

Then Allie said, "Mr. Brauny, I'm sure our viewers would like to know what kinds of supplements or drugs you may have, or may not have taken as a child or early in your career."

Then Max understood. He said, "It's a cocktail really. Most of it you can buy over the counter, some of it by prescription."

Machen looked like someone trying to stay calm while his ass was on fire. Allie said, "What are the ingredients?"

With the camera panning in on Max, he recited a list of ingredients and their amounts.

The camera then panned in on Allie Machen for a closeup. He looked into the camera and oozing sincerity, he said, "Folks, remember that you heard it here first."

The first caller was livid. "You rotten bastard! Now every kid in the country will be using that formula. You've destroyed everything I hold dear!"

"Well," Max said, "it will definitely enhance their performance." The next caller tried to be serious but he couldn't stop laughing. He said, "Look, I'm a pharmacist. If they take that formula their performance will be enhanced all right, but I can tell you that it won't be much fun. That formula you gave, everything in it's a laxative. Why'd you do it?"

"I agreed to come on The Allie Machen's show *on the condition* that the subject of performance enhancing drugs would not come up. Mr. Machen double-crossed me, so I thought, *OK, you want to get down and dirty? OK then. Let's get down and dirty!*"

Max then rose up out of his chair and said, "Sister Mary Beth works with the developmentally disabled. Send my check to her. I'm out of here."

Allie Machen called. All choked up, he said, "Buddy boy, you used my show, my career, to wipe your own ass."

"I sure did! So what kind of drugs are you taking. You tried a double-cross and it backfired. You had to be loaded to try pulling that one off!"

That was the last time anyone ever asked Max about performance-enhancing drugs.

• • •

Josie Gilmore called. How she got his number Max did not know. "Max," she said, "whatever you think of me, you know I'm not a thief. Can you believe it, I'm in jail. It's all a big mistake. If you could straighten this out I'd be ever so grateful."

He asked himself, *what is it about me that attracts crooked women?* What he said was, "Who's your arresting officer?"

"Detective Costello."

"I'll see what I can do."

• • •

Detective Costello, at the King County Courthouse, looked guarded and said, "Mister Brauny, what can I do for you?"

"Josie Gilmore. She's coming on to me, all breathy, sounding needy and sincere."

"That why you're here?"

"Since she called me, I'm wondering if somehow she's planning to connect me to whatever it is she's done."

"You here to help her?"

Max's eyes went wide and he slowly shook his head. "I'm here to cover my ass. I don't trust that girl. I suspect she called me to hook me into whatever it is she's done."

"Relax. There's no chance. You didn't get it from me, but she's been buying expensive items, returning to the store with her receipt, and taking the same item off the shelf and returning it for a refund. She's ripped off local stores for plenty . . . says she spent it all on drugs, and doesn't have a dime left."

"Detective, I went to school with that girl, and she's careful about what she puts in her body. She won't touch even carbonated drinks or sweets, much less drugs."

Max then gave Costello two game tickets.

• • •

Josie was wholesomely attractive, was white, well-spoken, and came from what's known as a 'good' family. She got the Judge she wanted and was placed on a monitored house arrest while awaiting a delayed sentencing. Josie then disappeared while leaving the ankle monitor behind.

Max thought, *have I seen the last of Josie Gilmore? God, I hope so. That girl scares me.*

Chapter Nine—Max is Arrested

Max's bat caught fire in his third year in the Majors and he was leading the league in extra base hits. Also, for a short time, too short, he connected with Annie Schiff. She said, "You're body's tight like a drum. I could light a match off you. How do you do it? You eat more than any man I ever saw, and there's not an ounce of fat on you. What's your secret?"

"No secret. I work my ass off. I drink only non-alcoholic beer and beginning a month after season's end, two days a week I work out with my mother's barbell. I do some heavy lifts first and then shift down to 200 pounds, that's bird weight for me, and I work up a good sweat doing the clean and jerk lift. Off-season Rabbit, Johnny Red, and I keep loose hitting each other grounders, flyballs, and taking our turns in the batting cage."

This day Laura Warrren arrived with her father. She shook the hand of Johnny Red, shook Max's hand and then retreated with her sketch pad to a seat in the shade.

Rabbit said, "She's a professional artist, talented, does illustrations and caricatures, and intends to memorialize us this day. Her mother's white, we separated shortly after Laura was born, and she divorced me when Laura was two. My daughter doesn't trust ballplayers."

Max looked at Laura and said, "You don't trust ball players?"

"I trust you to be the charming children you are. You go into the candy store, sample the goods, and leave without paying. Not, I might add, that anyone ever complains."

Max looked to Rabbit and said, "She really does know who we are." Looking back to Laura he said, "You're smart as hell and you're gorgeous."

"My father is the handsomest man in the world and a charmer. You move well, you're different, unhandsome, and not at all what I'd call charming. Other than that, you're just like him. I'm not about to take on a muscle-bound child and try to make a man out of him."

• • •

"Max looked to Rabbit, and said, "Your daughter, she can get pretty frosty."

"She has reason. Her mother convinced her that I was cheating on my wife during her pregnancy and divorced me. That left my daughter without a father."

Max's eyebrows went up. "You saying you *didn't* cheat on her?"

"I did not."

"Jesus."

• • •

They lost the World Series in their last game at Yankee Stadium. In New York, the city of Max's youth, his birthplace, there had been a smattering of boo's and cheers when he came up to bat.

He had not seen Miff or Girt for years but he had mailed them World Series Tickets. After the series, Max talked to them by phone while waiting to board the team flight back to Seattle.

He had no idea that he had already played his last game of baseball.

• • •

Detective Wolff showed up . . . again. Max said, "What is it this time?"

"Annie Connelly, you dated her, and now she's missing. Also, Betty Bolen says you agreed to pay her $5,000 to kill your mother and that you never paid. She says she's willing to testify to this in return for a reduced sentence. You have anything to say to this?"

"You here to arrest me?"

"Later."

• • •

Four days later Detective Wolff, backed by three uniformed Seattle Policemen, arrived at Max's home. They cuffed him, booked him in the King County Jail, arraigned him, and read him his rights. He was fingerprinted and isolated in an interrogation room. An hour later Detective Wolff arrived. He said, "You know why we're here so let's not waste each other's time. Constance Roth, where is she?"

Max could hear the confusion in his own voice when he said, "Who the hell is Constance Roth?"

Wolff wasn't buying it. In a voice dripping with contempt, he said, "You know who, the thirteen year old you've been diddling."

• • •

The Very Reverend Roth was the picture of moral integrity, of nobility, a dignified man with a tidy mustache—he had witnessed Max's poster picture hanging in the bedroom of his thirteen year old daughter. He reported that when he questioned his daughter, crying, she admitted to having had intercourse with Max Brauny.

"For her own protection," Reverend Roth said, "I locked her in her bedroom but when I returned with her meal tray she was gone."

The veracity of the Reverend Roth's report went unquestioned.

The Investigators assumed that Constance Roth had crawled out her bedroom window, moved along the roof to a tree she could climb down, and that Max was either hiding her . . . . or hiding her body.

The Redmond police and cadaver dogs tore Max's house and property apart looking for Constance Roth. Later, after the forensic team left, someone torched his house and car.

Max was in lockup while the Police and his insurance company assumed Max had ordered the torching to destroy physical evidence of Constance Roth having ever been in his car or home. The purple press leaped on the suspicion that he had first debauched and then destroyed Constance Roth.

Yesterday's hero became today's pariah. The team was in turmoil. Was it true? They didn't know what to think."

Max was still in lockup when he was served with a restraining order forbidding his teammates from having contact with him.

When Rabbit Warren was asked to sign that restraining order he said, "I want no part of this and I'm retired."

The others, including Johnny Red, signed the restraining order..

• • •

Arthur was a digger—he dug. His mother was a Wheaten Terrier, his sire was unknown. A friendly puppy, when he was moved in with mature cats Cassy and Polly, they quickly taught him the wisdom of keeping his distance. As he grew older and larger a truce was established and when a stray cat came through the cat door it was Arthur who cornered the cat and gave them a fierce barking. Miss Larson would then drag Arthur away and allow the cat to make their escape.

In his declining years, Arthur had ridded the neighborhood of moles—digging them up and laying them lovingly on Miss Larson's doormat—where they died of fright.

His most notable achievement was uncovering the body of young Constance Roth.

• • •

District Attorney Mason came to see Max. He said, "There is this neighborhood dog, Arthur I think his name is. He's Miss Larson's Wheaten Terrier. Arthur dug down in the Reverend Roth's rose garden and uncovered Constance Roth's body. The landscaper, seeing the body, called 911. Constance Roth had been wrapped in two plastic garbage bags. The autopsy revealed the dust in the garbage bags was the same dust contained in her lungs. Her injuries were consistent with a fall and she was a virgin and still breathing when she was buried.

• • •

Max had to sit down. . . . . District Attorney Mason shook his head and said, "That dog must love you."

Gathering himself, Max gasped, "He loves you, not me. I can prove it."

"How?"

"Tomorrow morning, you take Arthur and your wife and lock them in the trunk of your car, then drive them around all day. Night time, unlock the trunk and then see which one kisses you. Then, for sure, you'll know who loves you."

Max's insurance carrier had initially refused to pay off on his house and car. After his exoneration they were forced to pay up. Max severed all ties with that company.

· · ·

Reverend Roth was asked to report to the Police Station. Being civic-minded, he did so. When questioned, he reported that Mr. Max Brauny may not have been entirely responsible for what happened. He admitted that his daughter, unfortunately, had taken after her mother's side of the family and was a bit of a Jezebel, as was her mother.

Nothing shook the Very Reverend Roth's dignity. He was interviewed and tested by Police Psychologist Dr. James, PhD., who then interviewed Reverend Roth's ex-wife. She too reported that her ex-husband was delusional, and that, other than for procreation, she had never been interested in sex and had been celibate since her daughter's birth.

Locked up on the Psych Ward—Reverend Roth volunteered to conduct church services and provide patients with the spiritual guidance he saw they so obviously needed. His dignity, his quiet humor, upright appearance, and humane manner, would have led a visitor to assume that he was the doctor and the one in charge. Ironically, the patients on the ward proved to be less vulnerable to seduction by this man, than were some of the mental health professionals. It was agreed, however, that this man was delusional and therefore dangerous.

· · ·

Detective Wolff said, "Well, you got away with it Max. Damn shame. With the Reverend Roth's commitment there's not enough evidence to bring you to trial for the diddling of his daughter."

• • •

When Max showed up at the stadium he was met by General Manager Andy Schott.

"I can't tell you," he said, "how relieved we all are to know that you've been cleared. Your suspension has been lifted and the sooner we can get you back on the field the better." Waving his hands for emphasis, he said, "We took out that Restraining Order only to protect the team."

"I seem to remember having been a member of that team. So what did you do to protect me?"

Andy Schott dropped his eyes—"Can't wait to get you back—say something please!"

Looking in his locker, Max said, "The pictures of my mother, where are they?

General Manager Schott raised his hands palms up, said, "We don't know what happened to them."

For Max, that was the final straw. Baseball was over—.

Chapter Ten—An Actor Prepares

Max phoned Miff and Girt. Miff picked up. She yelped, "It's Max! Holy shit! You were our best friend and we've missed you. You've been a hero one day and a villain the next. God! That has to have been rough . . .. We've moved from Eleventh. We're living at 72 Bank Street. We'd love to see you and we have plenty of room."

There was an eagerness in Miff's voice and Max choked up, looked in the mirror and seeing his own sorrowful expression, he thought, *you've really missed those two.*

Some in the media had been quick—too quick—as it turned out, and grateful for the opportunity to declare, "I always knew there was something wrong about that guy."

• • •

Taking his time on the drive to New York, when he arrived, Max found a parking spot on Bank Street, took off his shades, and knocked on the door at 72 Bank. Gert answered the knock. She hollered over her shoulder, "It's Max." Miff came out of the kitchen and they all hugged. Max thought, *Damn this feels good!* He said, "It's nice seeing you two again."

Later that evening, sitting over a decent table wine, Miff said, "Still no woman in your life?"

"Nada. Nothing. Zippo. Let's change the subject."

Gert tossed her head. "Your teammates signing that restraining order, that was shitty."

"They did. The baseball I loved . . . and now my boyhood friend Johnny Red . . . now it all tastes like vinegar."

• • •

When Max visited Miff and Gert's Coffee Shop he was stunned by the vitality, the clarity in Gert's readings. Gert's poetry readings were well attended. In the time he had been gone, the emotional power, the clarity and her rendition of the poetry of others, had become legendary.

He chased down Reginald McNally, the acting teacher Gert told him about . . . although 'chased down' is a misnomer. Reggie is crippled with arthritis and lives in his wheelchair. Forty years old he is unable to leave his apartment without help, and like a seashell cast up on the beach, he sits stranded—a young/old sea conch.

Reggie asked, "What do you read?"

"The sports page, the funny papers, biographies, history. I like the flow of Shakespeare's language. Plus, the way I look, girls seeing me reading Shakespeare, it sometimes gives them the impression I might be an intellectual."

Reggie said, "Heaven forbid they think that. Go to my bookcase for the copy of Hamlet, turn to Act One, Scene Two and read the soliloquy that starts with: Oh, That this too too solid flesh would melt."

"Don't need to. Know it."

With raised eyebrows, McNally listened to his delivery. He looked surprised, said, "You have a natural rhythm in your speech— there are many fine actors with true emotion yet they lack that rhythm. You won't find them onstage doing Shakespeare, except perhaps badly."

"There is also a sense of emotional rigidity, a guardedness, a re- pressed rage in your delivery, a rage that I suspect has been triggered by recent events in your life. So, we need to stick a jumper cable up your ass to jumpstart your emotional battery and reach for other emotions. Max, was there ever a time in your life when you might have welcomed your own death?"

He nodded. "Several. What comes to mind is the day I took the subway to Coney Island with my mother's ashes, poured Mom's ashes into the waters—I thought about drifting out to sea with her—."

"Okay," Reggie said, "in your mind, relive the scene. Relive the memory of gathering your mother's ashes and walking to the subway.

He did. "Where," Reggie said, "are you now?"

"Eight Street and Sixth Avenue."

Reggie walked Max through every step of the way right up to the moment he released his mother's ashes. Reggie said, "Now deliver the first six lines."

"Oh! That this too, too, solid flesh would melt,
Thaw, and resolve itself into a dew!
Or that the Everlasting had not fixed His canon 'gainst self-slaughter.
Oh God, God,
How weary, stale, flat and unprofitable
Seem to me all the uses of this world!"

"Good," Reggie said, "Hamlet's world weariness has replaced your rage. Again, do the scene from the top, flatten your voice on the word flat, and this time play Hamlet's world weariness with more vigor."

This sounded like a contradiction, but Max did it. After delivering the last line of that soliloquy he was emotionally drained.

Reggie said. "Better. Now give me $100, go home, work on that soliloquy and come back the same time next week."

Once a week for the next three months, Reginald McNally and Max worked on Hamlet's soliloquies. Reggie was a tyrant—a bully. From his wheelchair, as if with a hot poker, he reached down inside and forced Max to re-experience and use every miserable and not-so-miserable moment in his life. It worked. It added color and depth to those lines.

• • •

Something else was going on. Max took another look and said, "Miff, are you pregnant?"

Miff and Girt started giggling. "Yes. We wanted a baby so I slept with a friend of ours, a blond young man, for thirty nights."

"Uh huh. How was that for you?"

"It was pleasant. It was friendly—but there wasn't a lot of sizzle."

. . .

Reginald McNally demanded everything Max had, and then went for more. To shift gears emotionally and make the transition from one feeling state to another had been laborious, had taken forever, but, by the end of four months, thanks to McNally's coaching, transitions from one emotional state to another had moved from labored to instantaneous.

. . .

"Reggie, everybody talks to me about playing Lenny in a revival of Steinbeck's 'Of Mice and Men.' Someday I might want to play *Macbeth*. Is there some way we could work with other actors on *Macbeth*?"

Reggie said, "I'll make some calls—see what I can do. There are good actors out there who never get anything but walk on parts." He paused, looked speculatively at Max and said, "There's no one in the world looks like you. You've been hitting the weights plus you have talent—maybe you can't hit baseballs anymore, but as an actor you have an innate talent and you will find work. "Broderick Crawford was brilliant as Lenny in Steinbeck's play 'Of Mice and Men' and for the rest of his career he fought against that muscle-bound and simple typecast. You're right that playing the part of Lenny early in your career would leave you forever type-cast."

. . .

In time, but not yet, Max and Frank Grady would become friends. But for now, one of his classmates, also from Seattle, was Frank Grady's eldest son Cody Tyler.

After class, they went off to have coffee. "Rumor has it," Max said, "that your father is a man once lived with a wife and two mistresses and that he's a gangster."

"You're not very good at making friends are you Max."

Shaking his head, he said, "Not good at all, and I have a world of people out there that are afraid of me."

"Dad," Cody said, "does a little better than that. As a kid he was being raised by his grandfather, lost him same as you lost your mother, and as an adult, Dad was shot by Ricco Juliano and then Dad put a bullet through Ricco's heart.

The FBI spent two years and a ton of money trying to connect Dad with the murder of Adele Yonkey. The pressure drove our mothers to take me, my sister Alsana and my brother John into exile in Switzerland; that was where my brother Wassef was born.

"Eventually, a Mister Wayne Phillips was found guilty of killing Adele Yonkey and our father was exonerated."

"Sounds like my story."

"It does. All that negative shit about Dad is in the public record. All the positive shit, and there's a ton of that too, is not in the public record. Mark Antony said:

The evil that men do lives after them.

The good is oft interred with their bones

So let it be with Caesar.

"As a child," Cody said, "and living in Switzerland, I spoke French, Spanish, and Arabic as well as English, and I had a number of kid parts in French and Italian films.

• • •

Another of their classmates was Fay Rodale. She was black, beautiful, and talented. Everything she did was good but Reggie wanted more, especially in Act 5 Scene 1 where Lady Macbeth says: "Will these hands ne'er be clean."

Reggie said, "Let's do an improvisation."

Reggie took Max aside and said, "In this scene you have admired Fay from a distance since you and Fay were teenagers. You have decided that, class and race be damned, she is the girl you want. As a first date you want to take her water-skiing. So that she will feel safe, you tell her she could bring her little sister along if she likes."

Then he took Fay aside. "Fay, in this scene you are a beautiful but poor black girl living in a one-room shanty with your parents and your thirteen-year old sister. When you were the same age as your sister you had been used and discarded by a rich white man. You recognize that this son-of-a-bitch, the son of that same plantation owner, is now out to nail your little sister's thirteen-year-old black ass."

Reggie had no way of knowing he had accurately reported Fay's early history. Bringing them together, Reginald said, "Max—Begin."

"Fay, we've never spoken even though I've seen you and your little sister around since we were children. I'd like to know you and your sister, starting by taking the two of you water-skiing."

"I know you would."

"It would be good, getting to know you better."

"It would be good for you Max. Since you've already screwed every white girl in the County between ages of thirteen and twenty, and now you want to screw all the little black girls as well!"

Max was stunned—Reginald snapped, "Keep going."

Fay exploded. "You think my little sister would feel honored to fall on her back and have you fuck her?" She shouted, "Look at you Max! You're a pervert and a fucking freako, some kind of a freak that should have died out a thousand years ago! You should be extinct!"

Max felt his pecker shrivel. Fay's reliving of her early history had pushed her way-way over the line and even she looked shocked. Both hands covered her mouth and nose she said, "Oh God! Oh God! I'm so sorry Max! I could kill myself for saying those horrible things!"

In the stunned silence, Reginald thundered, "Stay with the guilt! Now play your guilt through Act 5 Scene 1!"

She did. That scene came alive. By the time Fay did the line: *Will these hands ne'er be clean,* a cold shiver was coursing through the room. But Fay had gutted Max. She said, "I feel awful. I am so sorry Max!"

Max walked out the door.

Chapter Eleven—Football

Max, living on the west coast, had never even heard of arena football. He learned it was definitively minor league and was played in tiny indoors arenas throughout the Midwest.

Max located a gentleman now retired from his position as equipment manager for a pro football team. He agreed to procure well-fitted and top quality football pads, helmet, shoes, and two uniforms subject to being colored as necessary, plus everything else needed.

A St. Louis paper carried the announcement of one of those cattle calls scattered throughout the Mid-West euphemistically referred to as a "pro football tryout." Truth is, paying sixty bucks a head, about sixty of the areas athletes will show up at these events to run some 40s, run the cones, do bench presses and catch a few passes with the hope that this tryout might lead to a contract to play arena football.

Max showed up at one of the tryouts supposedly as an observer. Seeing Max, one of the tryout sponsors got on the phone and tipped off sportscaster Mike Owens that Max Brauny, formerly with the Seattle Mariners prior to his false arrest, was now looking to play arena football. Everyone looked when Max walked through the door. They always did. Max had been hitting the weights and had bulked up to 210 pounds, was short, but the broadest man in football. Now, even more than before, he looked like a fantasy comic book character.

• • •

Sportswriter Mike Owens said, "Mr. Brauny, as a former major league baseball player, why are you here?"

"I'm looking around, looking for something to do."

"Is this because your former teammates signed that No Contact Restraining Order against you?"

"My mother wanted me to play football— football wanted me to play football—I should have listened."

"You sound bitter."

"Do I? I'm looking around. Maybe I'll play football."

• • •

Max acquired the brochure for the Great Lakes Indoor Football League and visited almost every team. Of those visited, Rochester Minnesota had the best facility and most successful franchise.

At the Club in Harrisville, Minnesota, forty players were milling about, pissed and debating whether to even suit up. The owner of the Club, former used car salesman Honest Tom Baily, had skipped town with the ticket money while leaving behind a ton of promises, unpaid bills, and a room full of hurt. After each of the players had given expression to their outrage, Eddy Hays, the Harrisville Whackers 32 year old quarterback and team coach spoke up. "Guys," he said, "We've been had and we're not going to get paid. We could leave now and those fans who have paid to see this game could tear up this arena. All we have now is this one game. I say let's do it."

That's all they had. They played their hearts out and the Harrisville Whackers, Eddy's team, lost badly.

Major League baseball and football is all about winning. It seemed to Max that arena football was about giving it your best shot. Max saw something both pathetic and yet heroic in this.

When the players came out of their showers and were dressed, Max provided each player from both teams with a check for $150.

Max approached Coach Eddie Hays and said, "Coach, I have millions. If you're willing to stay on as Owner, Coach and General Manager, then I'll bail out this team. I see four things you need— make that five. That piece of shit you call the team bus has got to go. You need a bus with seats that recline so the players can rest coming and going. You need to get bids from general contractors on fixing up the arena and the playing field needs a decent padded surface. You need new uniforms, those you have look like shit, you need a draw, and that's me. I always draw a crowd."

Coach Eddie Hays sat down. Looking up he said, "You have the offensive lineman's build that coaches dream of finding but never do because there's no one else like you in this world. I have to say that even if we find you can't play football, spectators will show up just to see you make an ass of yourself."

• • •

Denny Bendiksen was the best lineman Hays could find to work Max out. Tuesday Denny Bendiksen lined up against him. This was not high school football. Fueled by the rage of recent events, it took Max a few plays to get his self under control and focused on what and why he was doing this, and the evening sports news had shots of former baseball great Max Brauny putting professional defensive tackle Benny Bendiksen on his back.

• • •

"Coach," Max said, "Since quitting baseball I've been hitting the weights and I'm feeling mean enough to enjoy knocking down big linemen, but I'm not feeling mean enough to enjoy running over people."

"You want line play."

"I want line play."

"Line play in Arena Football is about as pure as it can get. There's not enough room to do stunts. You were a center in high school so I'll start you at center. You have the quintessential offensive lineman's build—the build that coaches dream of finding but never do because there's no one else like you."

• • •

That first game was really something. Nobody got past Max on pass plays. By the second quarter, on running plays, he was taking out both a lineman and sometimes a linebacker. The field is short and there's a lot of scoring in Arena Football—they won 59 to 49.

Coach Hays had a field day— threw six touchdown passes and no interceptions—they were on the way to filling the arenas.

• • •

For those who retain fond memories of the comradeship, the team spirit of the one for all, all for one they found in High School Football, expecting to find something akin to that in this tough underbelly of professional football, they will find they have entered a different world. Two things mitigate against the establishment of closeness within a team. First, that guy playing beside you this week will very likely be gone next week. If not them, probably it's you who will be gone. Second, everybody is watching for any sign of vulnerability or softness, and when they find it they are merciless.

For others it felt cool to be a part of pro football even in the little ways—the crowds, the music, the autographs seekers.

• • •

Game two Max felt more comfortable, could read the defense better, they had three new faces in the lineup and the stands were full; the game was sold out. Two of the Whackers had signed their first pro contract minutes before the game. They won by a lopsided score.

His former Baseball Agent had garnered Max a decent baseball contract but Max had not appreciated the agent's response to his arrest . . . Johnny Red had also dumped that agent.

Max signed up with Agent Bernie Blare."

Bernie, as a prospective agent, had been lied to and manipulated by college athlete's and their parents; he had been rebuffed at every turn but now, his having signed Max Brauny, they came to him.

Bernie filmed every play. Those films were revealing. The thing is, in arena football, coaches and teammates won't help you with feedback on your technique; that would be going soft. It's sink or swim. Either you make the play or you don't. However, they do let you know about mental errors.

Each game, there were new faces in the lineup. The only players not subject to being replaced were Eddie Hays at quarterback and Max Brauny at center.

• • •

"At seasons end Max rented a house in the woods out by Ho-quam, Washington. The ocean was not far and there was a steep hill behind the house that rose up about 50 yards. Early morning, while it was still cool, he did runs, as fast as he could, up that hill. Late afternoon, he'd do grass up-downs, agility drills, and lift weights. His barbell was custom-made and would hold 700 pounds. Presently, he was doing 600 pounds in the bench press, and without a spotter. By the years end he expected to bench 700 pounds.

Chapter Twelve—Meet Hal Kempler

Max was in Hoquam and doing his shopping when a medium sized and well-put together Asian man accosted him. He said, "My name is Mister Cho. Your father wishes to see you." He handed over two airline tickets, one was for round trip flights between Seattle and Seoul, Korea and the other ticket was for round trip flights between Seoul and Bangkok, Thailand.

• • •

Hal Kempler, as a young man, had shipped out as a stoker on a coal burning cargo ship. He had been in a Manila bar when a Seaman from a Navy ship, thinking it funny, bit off the nipple of a prostitute and then spit it out. Hal Kempler gathered up the offending Seaman while every other American made haste to vacate the area. When the first rioters arrived Hal flung the now sobbing Seaman to them and then followed bar girl Chi Chi in a circuitous back-alley route to her cousin who was in the drug trade.

And so it was that Max's father-to-be exited the Philippines and embarked for Southeast Asia.

• • •

Sitting alone at the Sea Tac Airport, Max listened to the two gentlemen behind him. Both of them were in their sixties and they were reliving the glory of having played on the same High School Team with Vonzell, who later went on to have a decent four year pro football career. He was a legend to them. The two gentleman who had played alongside Vonzell. After all those years, they still felt pride in having been a part of that legend.

He thought about that during his flight to Seoul. For the first time he understood that when he too became a legend, those playing beside him also became a part of the legend.

And, when it was thought Max had committed that terrible crime, it destroyed their legend as well. Now, with his innocence being reestablished, the legend was being revived and he recognized that being even a small part of the legend can warm the bones for a lifetime.

•   •   •

Max had cleared Thailand Customs and Immigration when a tiny creature jumped in front of him and forced him to halt. "Hey big boy," she said. "I shine your shoes, suck your cock same time."

"Later," he said as he stepped around her and ran the gauntlet of taxi drivers, took the train, and then caught a water taxi and floated into Bangkok.

He saw Mr. Cho cross in front of him from about thirty feet ahead. Cho ducked into a doorway—Max followed, Cho locked the door and the two of them went out the back door and started running.

When Max spoke of it, he said, "We ran about two miles. With my bulk, and in that humid heat, plus my carrying case and having to dodge to avoid running over someone, that two mile run was tough. By the time we entered the boat, sweat was pouring off me and I was dehydrating. Cho had hardly taken a deep breath. Then the monsoon rains came, and that cooled me off. We motored through the night and I couldn't have told you whether we were traveling upstream or downstream. With daylight I recognized we were traveling upstream.

•   •   •

On the third day we docked and began the trip through the

jungle. Mid-day we arrived at a compound with about ten acres of lawn and a luxury home in the middle. Very little men with very large automatic weapons were in strategic positions. My father, Hal Kempler, and his wife, May Ling, were waiting on the veranda.

• • •

When we were seated, my father took two deep breaths and said. "I sent for you because, having been a heavy smoker all my life, my lungs are shot and I don't have much time. My wife was fifteen when her parents were executed by the Khmer Rouge. She escaped to Bangkok and went to work in the brothel where I found her."

I looked to May Ling.

"The other women were nice and the customers were usually nice. Then your father came along, he was so big. The other women assured me he was a good customer and that I could do this."

"You could?"

"I could." Then with a twinkle in her eye she said, "I did."

Max's father said, "I'm dying . . . I wanted to see you before I died. I have loved only two women in my life, your mother and May Ling. I'm tired now. I'm going to bed."

• • •

For nine days Max spent time with his father and watched his labored breathing. On the tenth day May Ling and Max were in attendance when his father's breathing stopped—no drama, it simply stopped.

May Ling asked to be left alone with her husband.

When May Ling came out of the room she handed Max a letter.

My dear Son,
I do not regret the life I chose. I regret leaving you now. I regret having had to leave your mother. Even at this distance, I have bled with the injustices you suffered and rejoiced in your triumphs. Seattle Attorney Mayo Longstreet is the Executor of my Last Will and Testament and will arrange your inheritance.
My boyhood friends, Mr. Donnie Hill and his wife Alice,

have a daughter who has suffered an injustice. I charge you in my absence, along with notifying Donnie of his inheritance, to right the wrong done to his daughter. If you need assistance in this undertaking, I advise you to contact Mr. Chuck Devane in Boston. I have done business with him for many years and he is trustworthy.

I have already provided for the others. I want my ashes dumped in Boston Harbor.

Your father, Hal Kempler

May Ling, said, "You go to Bangkok and wait for me there. I will bring your father's ashes. Then you fly back to Seattle."

"What about you May Ling?"

"I have responsibilities, a business to run."

Chapter Thirteen—To the Rescue

Max landed at Sea Tac Airport and the evening sun provided a welcome. He paid bills, answered mail, took care of business, and then, with his father's ashes, he flew to Boston, rented a car and as requested, poured his father's ashes into Boston Harbor. He choked up—first his Mom's ashes, now his Dad's.

On arrival in Fitchburg, Massachusetts, he located the current home of his father's boyhood friend, knocked on the door, and it was opened by Donnie Hill. "Max Brauny. Seeing your picture on the sports page we always thought you had to be related to Hal Kempler. And now you're here." Stepping away from the door he said, "Please come in." Turning, he raised his voice saying, "Alice, we need you."

Alice, seeing Max from the doorway to the living room, stopped cold. Her mouth dropped open. "Oh my God!" she said, "It's like seeing a ghost. Is Hal your father?"

Max nodded, "Was. Cancer got him."

"Oh God. I'm so sorry to hear that. Hal was our best friend. When Donnie and I married, Hal was the Best Man at our wedding, wished us well, went to sea, and that's the last we ever saw of him. We thought he must be dead."

• • •

Donnie and Max took seats in the living room and Alice served them coffee. Max said, "My father, preparing for the end, and tidying up the loose ends, as he called it, learned of the problem your daughter encountered. He charged me to address the problem, to right that wrong. I will need to know who did what and how many times."

Alice said, "Jenny won't talk about it. All she does is lay on her bed and stare out the window."

"What do you know?"

"Harvey Stanbrough invited Jenny to a teen party. He's the son of the richest man in Crestburg and he's the head of what's known as the Fabulous Three at the Crestburg High School." Alice dropped her eyes.

Seeing his wife unable to continue, Donnie said, "We were worried, then the guard at the Wilshire Gated Community called and said that Jennie was at the gate, looked pretty bad and that I better come and get her. We did. Right away, we knew she had been drugged and gang-raped. We took her to the hospital."

• • •

With Jenny's arrival at the hospital, the tears in the vaginal wall were treated, semen samples were taken, and it was determined that Jenny had ingested a potent drug cocktail. Within twenty-four hours the semen samples had disappeared.

Crestburg is a rich man's town. The town's only industry consists of clipping the stock dividends of those living within the Wilshire Gated Community. Those living within were inviolate while the lower town's economy was based solely on services to those who lived within.

Donnie Hill, as a supplement to his writing income, had been the caretaker of the private nine-hole golf course and its man-made pond. Now Donnie had been fired from that position and Chief Doggett of the Local Constabulary informed the Hill's that it would be to their best interest to vacate the town, and that if his daughter made any false allegations, she would be jailed and prosecuted for slander. Anything said or published on this matter would also be scrutinized for slander.

Max made some phone calls, informed the Hill Family that he

would be flying back to Seattle and would be back in a few days. He told the girl, "Jenny, when I get back you will need to talk to me. In order to fit the punishment to the crime, to get those bastards, I need to know the details, who did what. I don't need this just yet, but I will need it when I get back, and you will give me that. I can't give you justice, but what I can give you is a sweet-assed revenge. We're going to take those assholes down!

"Also," turning to Donnie, he said, "my father wanted you to have this."

He handed Donnie a certified check. Donnie was stunned. Alice stood looking over his shoulder, as did his daughter. They continued to read and reread the certified check for $500,000.

• • •

Frank Grady met Max when he came off the plane, drove him to his home on Mercer Island and they talked well into the night. Frank said, "Dee's going to love this. A corrupt, paid for, and delivered Police Chief." By cellphone, Frank reached FBI Agent Dee Dixon. Frank entered one of the back bedrooms and closed the door. Re-entering the living room, Frank said, "It's good. She'll be on it with you and she's someone you'll like."

• • •

Jennie Hill said, "There were six girls and seven boys from the hill. I was the only one from the flat at that party. The drink they gave me was doped up and I became dizzy and feeling feint.

'Harvey Stranbrough was at my side, and led me into the tent and laid me up on the table. "The last thing I remember before passing out, was one of the other girls sticking her head through the tent flaps and snapping, 'We're leaving.'"

Jenny returned to consciousness and realized she was naked. "They took turns, those bastards, and when all the boys were through screwing me, they left."

• • •

Max paid a visit to the gentleman his father had spoken of. Chuck Devane was a large and red-faced gentleman with sharp intent eyes, was overweight and dressed in florid colors. He never agreed to anything, and Max never asked for anything. Instead, Max volunteered, "Wouldn't it be nice if they were to experience what they did to Jenny?"

Devane nodded, said, "Interesting."

• • •

Max was approached by two men and a good looking transsexual with breast implants. He would not have been able to testify to it, but they were apparently referred by Chuck Devane, and once again Max consulted with Frank Grady.

When he revisited Donnie Hill, Max said, "Donnie, I strongly suggest you take your family for a month's vacation, and far away." Donnie took them to Puerto Rico.

Chapter Fourteen—Justice Served

Harvey Stranbrough was stopped at the red light when a car with the top down, and a beautiful woman driving, pulled up alongside him. She had luxuriant long dark hair and a spectacular bust. She said, "I'm lost. I would be ever so grateful if you would show me the way back to the Dew Drop Inn Motel."

Grinning, Harvey said, "Follow me." She did. When he pulled into the parking lot, she pulled in, parked in front of Cabin Number Ten and said, "Can I offer you some refreshments?"

"You can." She left the door ajar. Harvey parked and entered the cabin. Coming through the doorway, he was grabbed by a muscular set of arms from each side and the door was kicked shut. The woman said, "It's playtime."

Smiling, the beautiful woman stepped out of her skirt and panties. He saw that this supposed female had a very large dick.

• • •

Harvey's parents were appalled by the photos they received. "Why did you engage in such acts and why did you allow them to be taped?"

"I was raped by two at a time and with the third taking photos. They said that the photos were to ensure that I tell them the truth about who concocted and dosed Jenny with that drug cocktail; if what I told them proved to be true then the photos and negatives would be destroyed. They lied!"

"What did you tell them?"

"That it had been Mark Bryson who drugged her."

Harvey's father called the Bryson home. Mark was missing.

• • •

Mark had not suspected that the beautiful woman sitting next to him was not what she seemed. When he regained consciousness, he recognized he was nude, was gagged, and hands and feet were in padded restraints.

He heard a voice say, "He's awake now. Let's get him up on his feet." He was stood up and his restraints were tethered to two trees at the edge of the swamp. His three captors then retreated under mosquito netting, smoking, drinking, and playing cards. One of them said, "Those mosquitoes are feasting on doped up blood. What does a drunken mosquito look like?"

The other two laughed.

The transsexual said, "Maybe we should give him a drink of water?"

"The short one said, "With all those drunken mosquitos? Not me." The tall one echoed, "Me neither."

The transsexual sighed and said, "Okay, I'll do it."

She exited the mosquito netting, removed Mark's gag and he gratefully accepted a drink of water. Twice that night she gave him more water. The water was laced with LSD.

• • •

At daybreak Mark, freaking out and naked, was dropped off on the outskirts of Crestburg. After the first reported sighting, it took police six more hours to corral the nude, freaked-out and fleeing Mark Bryson.

• • •

Mark Bryson, Harvey Stranbrough, and Johnny Gibbs were the Fabulous Three at Crestburg High.

Harvey Stranbrough was in seclusion while Mark Bryson was

in a psychotic state from an excess of ingested psychedelics, and a quick recovery was not expected.

When Johnny Gibbs thought about this, the hair on the back of his neck stood on end. When school let out Johnny walked up to what he called his Chick Wagon. The Chick Wagon was Johnny's antique and fully restored 1939 Ford convertible. All the chrome was brand new, the seats were re-covered in new leather, the paint-job had been redone in a glazed yellow, and with red flames streaked back along the fenders.

Johnny was muscular, weighed 210 pounds and was infamous for his temper blowups. Teachers and students alike had learned not to cross him. Others were watching silently, and at a distance, as he walked up to the Chick Wagon.

Fifty gallons of raw chicken guts, heads, and feathers had been dumped into the front seat. All were waiting for the explosion to come. All, that is, save for a scar-faced old guy of more than fifty, who looked and laughed.

Howling, Johnny charged the old guy and threw a punch the old guy neatly slipped, staggered Johnny with a left hook, surgically broke Johnny's nose first from the left side, then again from the right. Johnny was whimpering, bleeding copiously, and his nose now pointed towards his ear. Then he was rolled in on top of the chicken guts.

Two Police officers with drawn weapons took the old guy, Frank Grady, into custody. He was mugged, finger-printed, stripped, issued a jailhouse orange jumpsuit, and booked.

The Police Chief, Amos Doggett, bald and potbellied, thumbs hooked in his gun belt, said, "Well, now, what do we have here? Some bad-ass with bullet scars on his gut, side and leg, knife-cut scar on his face, wearing a thousand dollar suit, rolls into town, beats up one of our local citizens, has a driver's license saying his name is Buddy Rich, but no other ID. When we do a name search for Buddy Rich we come up with nothing. No credit cards but one thousand dollars in crisp new $100 dollar bills."

Frank said, "$5,000 dollars in crisp new $100 dollar bills,"

"You just made another mistake boy. First mistake was coming to our fair town, second mistake was assaulting the son of a prominent citizen. Mistake number three is accusing this Police Department of corruption. Now that upsets me."

The old guy pulled down on his lower eyelid and said, "You see the tear in my eye? That's how sorry I am that you're upset. Now get me an attorney."

• • •

Newly anointed Attorney Orville Crane arrived. Tall, threadbare, and adam's apple working up and down, he plopped his briefcase down on the table and took a close look at the older man. "They think you're a real badass, had $1,000 in your pocket plus wearing a thousand dollar suit. They're peddling your description everywhere looking to connect you with other crimes. I'm amazed they haven't yet figured out who you really are."

Frank Grady chuckled, "Me too."

Attorney Crane was puzzled. He stared. "They haven't got your fingerprint checks back yet so time may be on our side. Possibly I can hurry this along, get you plea bargained down to a lower court and get you sentenced before they find out who you really are.

"Counselor, the last thing we need is to have this over quickly. My real name is Frank Grady, I'm Secret Service Retired, and what we have here is a situation of mass corruption. What you will do is get word to FBI Agent Dee Dixon that Frank Grady is in jail, and you will be the liaison between me and the FBI.

"They've got this big psycho kid in this town. He attacks people and gets away with it because his daddy's rich and owns the police department. The kid came after me, I busted him up some, and the cops in this town started pointing guns at me. That kid came at me like he is totally nuts—he belongs in a cage. FBI Agent Dee Dixon and her team are at the high School and hospital digging up the dirt, the assaults, the rapes and their cover-ups.

"Don't screw up! Slow down the process of getting me out of here!"

A smile, ever so slowly, replaced the amazement on the face of Counselor Crane, and awe in his voice, wide-eyed, he said, "A chance to fuck with the legal system. A lawyer's dream come true."

• • •

The State Police sirens could be heard from a long way off, arrived at the jail with sirens still blaring and FBI Agent Dee Dixon in the lead car.

Frank Grady was released.

Chief Doggett was stunned and mute, could only nod his head as he was being read his rights, driven away, and booked in another jail.

Agent Dee Dixon was a skilled interrogator and first played to Doggett's shock at being arrested, then skillfully, threw an admiring hook to his pride in having got away with so much and for so long. Chief Doggett could not help himself and his criminal pride prompted him to brag about a string of successful coverups to his receptive audience.

• • •

At the hospital, Nurse Windermere was truly frightened. *How much does FBI Agent Dee Dixon know?*

Agent Dixon, voice dripping like ice water, said, "Which is it going to be? Last chance you get to choose. We already know most of it. Either you will be charged as a co-conspirator and do the same amount of serious time as the others, they're going down whether or not you cooperate or, as a cooperating witness, you will be the one who chooses to receive a slap on the wrist as a cooperating witness. Last chance. You need to choose now."

Windermere broke her silence—and the crescendo followed—silences on all fronts evaporated.

It was also discovered that the wife of Deputy Dard had banked five of the $100 bills with consecutive serial numbers that had been taken off Frank Grady.

Deputy Dard was informed that the bills his wife had deposited were sequentially numbered and had been in the possession of Secret Service Agent Frank Grady, who, under the name Buddy Rich, had been placed under false arrest. On the advice of counsel, and with Deputy Dard joining Nurse Windermere as a cooperating witness, he received a reduced sentence.

Chief Doggett was sentenced to Cedar Junction Prison in Norfolk/Walpol. Frank said, "Don't take it so hard Amos. You being a crook like them, and yet rising to the rank of Police Chief, those other cons will be looking on you with nothing but respect."

Harvey Stanbrough, Mark Bryson, and Johnny Gibbs received four year sentences and were reunited with Chief Doggett in Cedar Junction. Then Johnny Gibbs hospitalized a fellow inmate, received an additional sentence for the assault, and was transferred to Maximum Security in Souza-Baranowski Prison in Lancaster.

The five girls got off light (way too light Max thought) and received suspended sentences as accessories after the fact, while the other boys received two year sentences.

• • •

Frank said, "Max, I'm getting too old for this. I'm flying to Mazatlan. Way back then, when Melina, Annette, Natalie and I vacationed in Mazatlan, it was the best time of our lives, and I want to see if I can recapture a piece of that moment."

• • •

Crestburg developed a new and lucrative industry in the filing of lawsuits. Attorney Crane was on the ground and running with the lawsuits, while Donnie Hill was writing an exposé of the malignancy that had been the Wilshire Gated Community.

Following the money, the evidence of past wrongs came out in the open. Those families living within could not fight back. All they could do was make out-of-court settlements, stall, and search for legal loopholes.

• • •

Max took satisfaction in having financed and set the wheels in motion, but it was Frank Grady who planned, got Dee Dixon of the FBI involved, and made the operation work.

Chapter Fifteen—Josie Gilmore

Max drove to New York for his first-time-ever meeting with Miff and Gert's baby daughter Marsha. She was a tiny, beautiful child with reddish brown hair midway between curly and wavy. Her skin tones and features provided light testimony to her African heritage.

Gert said, "Max, would you be willing to be Marsha's Godfather?"

"I'd be honored."

He loved Marsha on first sight and stayed with the three of them for four days. Then he flew back to Seattle. He needed a week of cooling off time before taking up the task of getting back in shape for football.

. . .

At Seahawk Headquarters, in a private screening, and with the entire coaching staff and management watching, Max was able to contain All-Pro David Sheehan's charges. Agent Bernie Blare said, "This is all friendly now but imagine what Max would be like if he had to sign with someone else and was lined up against the Seahawks."

. . .

Max returned to Hainsville and took Eddie and Phyllis out to the local steakhouse. Eddie said, "What are your plans Max? You planning to come back to the Hainsville Whackers?

"Can't. Bernie Blare set it up for me to bump heads with David Sheehan. He's Seattle's right guard and until I came along he was the strongest man in pro football. He can bench press 700 pounds. I prefer the quick lifts, the snatch and the clean & jerk. I'm younger than Sheehan, have a lower center of gravity, and I have the strongest legs in football."

"How did you do against Sheehan?"

"I stunned everyone, I was able to contain Sheehan's charges."

• • •

Max flew back to Seattle and drove to Aberdeen, up the coast to Neah Bay, and then across to Port Townsend. This town was different; so different, that he spent three days sometimes walking through the one- street downtown area, sometimes driving through the residential areas and viewing the unique architecture of its buildings. He thought, *whoever the architect was that designed and built these houses, he was having a good time.*

The open ambience of the town and its people felt good . . . so good that on foot he toured the towns restaurants and various places of business. The place he liked the best was the secondhand book store, but everything, including the people, felt relaxed and upbeat. He had to return to Seattle, but it occurred to him that Port Townsend would be a nice place to live.

• • •

Before each practice and before each game Max taped up using three kinds of tape, prewrap, hard tape, and soft tape to secure ankles, wrists, and every one of his fingers.

He was taping up for his first Seahawk practice when Donnie Lehane and other veterans dropped by to begin hazing the rooky sitting behind Max. Donnie said, "Rooky, it's time for you to stand up on that chair and tell us about you."

He did.

Lehane said, "Tomorrow Rooky, you will bring bagels and

donuts to the team before practice and I don't mean just any old dunking donuts."

Max was the only Rooky in camp exempted from the customary hazing of rookies.

• • •

He put in a call to Laura Warren.

"Hello?"

"Laura Warren?"

"Yes Max." "So. You recognized my voice. You left a message stating that you wanted to speak with me, that you owed me an apology."

"That was a month ago. I half hoped you might not call back. Eating humble pie is not my favorite dish."

"Understood."

• • •

Doorman Wally called up. "There's a young woman, Laura Warren, wants to come up and see you."

"Thanks Wally, Send her up."

• • •

"So," Laura said, "You have the penthouse." She walked over to the west windows. "You have a nice view over Puget Sound and the Olympics."

"I have coffee, iced tea, and lemonade. I'm afraid there's nothing alcoholic in the house. We can take seats facing the windows and catch the sun setting over the Olympics. I hate to say it, but you don't look well."

"I don't feel well, "Iced tea might help. I'm coming down with the flu or something so don't get too close. I asked my father if you would be plying me with drink and he told me you don't often use alcohol. The first time we met I accused you of having drank four or five beers already . . . and you never let on that you were dehydrated and the beers were non-alcoholic. Why?"

Max handed Laura an iced tea. The sun was beginning to set and the sky was tinting red. "You needed to believe I was a muscle-bound and irresponsible child, so why should I disappoint you. Besides, I was too damned tired to argue."

"Like me now. When those charges were brought against you I thought they were true and I raged against my father for having anything to do with you . . . I called you a monster that belonged in a cage. Then I found out you were innocent. That time we met in the airport you said I owed my father an apology for a lot more than that! What did you mean?"

Max sat down his coffee. This was a touchy subject. Staring out the window, he said, "You remember when the Reverend Roth accusing me of having sex with his daughter?"

"I do. You were innocent."

"And you remember the Very Reverend Roth had also accused the mother of his child of having had sexual relationships outside of the marriage?"

"I do."

"I've read the Court Transcripts and talked with the mother. She was as innocent as I was. Still, the Courts screwed up, ruled her an unfit mother and awarded Reverend Roth sole custody of their daughter. The good Reverend deprived the mother of her child, deprived the child of her mother, then deprived the child of her life."

Laura was not looking good. "Mom said that my father cheated on her while she was carrying me. You saying she lied? I never realized, not until this very minute. Oh God! Where's the bathroom? I'm going to be sick."

Laura knelt before the porcelain throne and let loose. Wiping her mouth, she said, "Get out of here Max. I'm about to let loose from the other end."

Too late. They heard it when her bowel let loose.

• • •

Max called 911, got her butt cleaned up and called her father. "Rabbit, I have an ambulance on the way here to pick up Laura. She's serious sick, I touched her forehead and she's burning up. I'll be getting her to Harborview."

• • •

The physician in charge said, "She has both urinary and intestinal infections. She's in shock, and we're taking her into Intensive Care."

Rabbit said, "Can I see my daughter?"

"Not now. We need to get her through the night and get her fever down. If we can do that, then she has a chance. Right now she's a very sick young lady and right on the edge."

Two PM the next day Rabbit was allowed five minutes with Laura. Seven PM he was allowed another visit.

This time Max went with Rabbit. Laura said, "Max, you wiped my shitty ass and put me in a clean pair of panties, then you got me to the hospital."

Rabbit looked at Max. "You wiped my daughter's ass?"

"I did. And I got to tell you she's got a sphincter back there strong enough —I think it could crack walnuts."

Rabbit's eyes opened wide and that broke the seriousness of the moment . . . both men laughed.

"I'm so glad," Laura hissed, "that you two men think my sphincter is something to laugh about.

"Max, I owed you an apology and now I owe you my life. But all the same, you're a rotten bastard Max. You enjoyed tearing me up."

"Maybe. You're the second woman to call me a rotten bastard. I was in Triple A when Kimmy entered the picture. She was taller than you, darker than you, a lot older, not nearly as good to look at, but she was a world-class con woman who could talk the birds out of the trees. She had her hand stuck down in my pocket while everything she said was a damn lie. I gave her the kiss-off and that's when she called me a rotten bastard for having wasted her time."

• • •

Max got playing time as the long snapper on special teams even in their first league game. Lou Holtzmann was the starting center when the Offensive Team took the field, but late in the fourth quarter, with the Seahawks ahead by two touchdowns, Max went in as the center for their last possession series. And that was the way it went for the first four games. Max was the special team's long snapper and late in the game, if the Seahawks had a comfortable lead, he was put in as the offensive team's center.

Starting center Lou Holtzmann never spoke to Max, not ever; not one word the entire season. He was traded off-season and Max began his second season as the starting center. When he screwed up, his teammates either dummied up or ridiculed him; only when he made a good play would they let up.

Their right guard, David Sheehan, was a silent, morose man who sat at the bar the night before each game until he was half in the bag. He hated women for some reason, definitely, he was not gay, but he did not like women. When on the field, it felt to Max as if in some non-verbal way Sheehan was telling him the things he needed to know.

Walking side-by-side off the field at game's end, Max said, "Sheehan, sometimes I get the feeling you're telling me something even though you don't open your mouth."

Max thought— *Back then, Neanderthals, only 15,000 of us and scattered all the way across Siberia, Israel, and Europe—so isolated from each other that we had no chance to develop language—we would have needed ESP just to find each other.*

• • •

Their early schedule was against the marginal teams and Max did have innate football instincts and made some good plays. His strength and lower center of gravity gave him leverage and wore down the opposing and bigger players— he was having a serious impact on the other team's defense—his position as a starter was solid.

Then, in Max's third year, nose tackle Charley Gates blew out his knee. They had two new candidates trying out at nose tackle. One was a big farmboy from Iowa named Rodney Hamilton. He stood 6' 6" tall and weighed in at 340 pounds. He would say, "All I do is throw the guard or center out of there and then go after the one with the ball, huh, huh, huh."

That boy had a one track mind. In practice Rodney couldn't throw either Max or David Sheehan out of there but he would keep trying even when the play had already swept by. With all his physical gifts and after four years of HS and four years of college, Rodney Hamilton could still barely read and write. Even worse, he couldn't read blocking patterns.

Rodney appeared surprised but not upset when he was cut and sent packing back to Iowa.

The other candidate, Davis, was their best special team player. On defense he was always in the right place at the right time, but not quite strong enough to move the pile in short yardage situations.

• • •

Max reported to Coach Manny Tisch's Office. Head Coach Tisch and Defensive Coach Darryl McNally were there. Coach Tisch said, "Max, we know your primary instinct is to protect rather than attack. The team has a problem. We haven't had much success at stuffing the run when our opponent needs only one or two yards for a first down. We need you at nose tackle in short yardage situations until we can get someone else who can stuff the run. Coach McNally and I both recognize that you are more suited to play on the offensive line and we want to keep you there. But at the moment the team needs a nose tackle who can stuff the run on short-yardage plays. We think you have the instinct and toughness a Nose Tackle needs."

"Why me? "Why not Sheehan?"

"If it was only for one game then Sheehan would be the logical choice. David Sheehan knows more about this game than you will ever know but he has taken hits for four years of high School, four more years of college, and eight years of pro ball. That's twelve more years of taking hits than you have. How many hits can his body take?"

"You playing on my heartstrings Coach?"

"Damn right I am! Some of our animals would make the world a safer place if they got in touch with their protective other side. On defense you will need to get in touch with your other side, the side of you that is an assaultive animal and wants to slap someone around. We think you can do this."

"Speaking about slapping someone around, my agent will be talking to you about more money."

• • •

"The lockers of defensive linemen and linebackers," Max said, "are minefields of funk and disorder. How they ever find what they need is a mystery. The lockers of offensive linemen are the exact opposite. Everything is in order with socks neatly rolled up and everything tidy and ready for inspection.

"A pro football team is a hotbed of practical jokes. It has to be. Otherwise the agony of endless meetings, practices, the viewing and reviewing of films would drive us all mad. The humor and the crudeness if not downright cruelty of some of the practical jokes is tempered to the five year old in each of us. It has to be. For those who have families, for six months of the year they spend more time with the team than they do with their families.

"In contrast to how neat and clean the lockers of the offensive linemen are, the cruelest and most offensive practical jokes are usually the invention of offensive linemen. The basic function of an offensive lineman is to protect, and while protecting, we take a hell of a beating; as protectors, we have to swallow so much anger that we need these practical jokes to keep from choking. Someone gets into someone's bathroom and craps in the holding tank of their toilet. Not only does this smell bad but flushing creates a real mess and smells even worse. One guy distracts you in the Shower while another is pissing on your leg. You don't know you're being pissed on because the Shower is also hitting you. It's a different world and these are some of the lighter practical jokes. Surprisingly, these practical jokes create bonding."

Chapter Sixteen—Laura Warren

The thing about baseball was that the heat and the daily grind left Max exhausted and took everything he had—as much as he loved the game—it was played in the hottest part of the year, and he was not built for baseball. The irony is that he had the perfectly designed body for an offensive lineman and even though he was not in love with the game, he was physically well-designed to deal with cold weather and to protect the quarterback. Other offensive lineman, after a tough win, would walk off the field with a strut in their step but when they hit the locker room, their adrenaline pump would shut down and they'd be so beat up there were times they needed an IV in order to shower, change clothes and make it to their car or the team bus.

When they lose a tough one it gets worse.

• • •

Max had returned to his condominium in Seattle when Rabbit Warren called. "Max, my daughter is devastated. She won't talk about it even to me. I know that somehow it relates to you but how? She won't tell me. Is there a third party involved?"

"Oh Jesus! If there's a third party involved I can guess who, has to be Detective Gunther Wolff. I have a whole scrapbook with names, dates, everything. Since I was 15 years old Gunther's been trying to nail me for something, and I've recorded it all. Rabbit, you drop the name of Detective Gunther Wolff on Laura and see what happens."

• • •

Rabbit called back. "You were right Max, Wolff showed my daughter a picture of you walking and holding the hand of a little girl, said they never found out who the girl was or what happened to her."

"Uh huh! Had to be Marsha Trotter. She's the only little girl I ever walked with and holding her hand. Her mothers are Miff Trotter and Gert Connery."

• • •

Max answered the phone. "Hello?"

"Max, it's Laura Warren. Can I come see you?"

"Goddamn, more than six months ago I called you, left messages. You never picked up and you never called back. You at Sea Tac Airport? I hear planes overhead, so catch a cab to my condo and I'll have dinners sent in."

• • •

Max answered the knock. Laura was wearing a green matching skirt and jacket. Her blouse was silky-white and her makeup and jewelry were perfect. "Laura. Come in."

"Thank you."

Their dinners arrived, and they were mostly quiet while having their evening meal. Laura couldn't finish her steak.

Max said, "You had a chip on your shoulder that first time we met."

"Two years on the couch has allowed me to forgive myself for the injustices I did my father—the injustices I did you—."

Max removed the plates. "I never heard Rabbit say an unkind word about your mother. Your mother seems to have gotten the free ride from everyone."

"What about me Max? Are you into giving me a free ride?"

"No free ride for you girl. When you least expect it I will rise up and bite you on the ass!"

"Well . . . Thanks for the warning."

"The first time I saw you I thought you were damn attractive. Then you came on like a real witch. How come?"

"You were so different, and yet I was attracted to that difference. Even now I can't imagine why."

Max shook his head saying, "Neither would anyone else."

"I wanted to bury my head in your chest. That scared me, and saying this in front of you scares me. I have images of you rolling over on me and smothering me. You're five foot seven and weigh 215. I'm five foot seven and weigh 105.

"Detective Gunther Wolff came to see me." She choked on the words, "He was really good. He spoke admiringly of how you were able to fool everyone, and how at age six you fooled the New York Educational system into providing you with eight years of private tutoring."

"And you believed him."

"Wolff shook his head in admiration of how you engineered the bank into having you arrested and then you shook the bank down."

"And you believed him."

"You keep saying that. He reeled off the names of maybe a dozen little girls who disappeared, they found only the body of little Constance Ross; she had been buried in her father's own rose garden, it couldn't be proven that it was you who planted her there, and then he showed me a picture of you walking with that little girl in hand. He said that this was probably the only mistake you ever made. He said they had shown that picture to a thousand people and not one could identify that little girl. Then he asked if I could identify her. I couldn't. Believing him was easier than not knowing what to believe."

"Wolff had to be desperate to try pulling that off."

"I suppose. Fortunately, my dad came to my rescue. He gave me the name Marsha Trotter. I looked her up, went to meet her, and she was the girl in the picture. Then I knew. Wolff was fabricating a case against you."

. . .

In a Court of Law, Judge Wilfred Mooney ruled, "This case troubles me—a former Police Officer conducting a fifteen year campaign of harassment and slander. Gunther Wolff, this Court finds you guilty and I sentence you to a term of no less than five years and no more than ten years. Bailiff, you will take the prisoner into custody. This Court is adjourned." The gavel came down.

"Finally," Max said, "I have Gunther Wolff off my ass."

• • •

The Seahawks made it to the playoffs with a record of twelve and four. They lost. Max was tired. He was tired of football—it wasn't his game but the more tired of football he was, the harder he worked at it—or was it the other way around? Maybe, he thought, *I'm just tired.*

Max told General Manager Lehane that this, his fourth year, would be his last. In the locker room, after the last season game, he said, "Guys, I was a baseball player. When baseball threw me out I was lost, dead inside. You guys are almost as ugly as I am, and maybe that's why my being a part of this team, I came alive again. You're a great bunch of guys, I thank you all, and I'm retired."

Chapter Seventeen—Meet the President

Max was driven to McChord Air Force Base and boarded a waiting jet. Frank Grady was the only other passenger. The hatch was closed, they fastened their seatbelts, heard the jets whine, and rumbled down the runway. Frank was still, hadn't said a word. Max was asking himself, *what the hell is going on.* Frank, as if reading his mind, muttered, "I don't know what's going on either."

October is not the best time to fly and they encountered more than a little turbulence on the flight to DC. Frank had drawn into a shell and was saying nothing. They landed at the Andrews Air Force Base and a stretch Limo with US Government plates rolled up.

Frank's old friends Agents Dennis Huff and John 'Cut'n Shoot' Cutter were there to meet them and they were grinning and exchanging insults with Frank Grady. This was something Max had never seen anyone else do with Frank Grady. He relaxed—some anyway.

Agent Huff said, "What we know is that there's an assassin out there planning to assassinate President Odie Knott when he gives his speech. We want Frank armed and to the right of the President and Max to the left of the President. If the need arises, Max, you're strong enough and it will be your job to remove the President to safety."

• • •

At a News Conference on the White House lawn, following the President's speech, reporters were wracking Press Secretary Barry Klems with demands. He waited for quiet. With the quiet Secretary Klems reported, "Our Intelligence has been good. We had known for some time that professional Hit Man Adali Sims had been commissioned to assassinate the President."

Another said, "Why wasn't the President informed of this?"

Secretary Klems snapped, "The President *was* informed of this! The citizens of this country put their trust in President Odie Knott to *lead*. The President felt it was his duty to present his social programs to the American people, put his trust in the Secret Service, and the Secret Service delivered; they took down Adali Sims approximately a hundred yards from where the president stood."

Senator Murchison leaped to the attack and demanded, "Why were experienced Secret Service Agents replaced with amateurs like Grady and Brauny."

Press Secretary Klems dropped his head, shook it slowly and raising his head and eyes upward, he coldly stated, "This is outrageous! Secret Service Agent Frank Grady is hardly an amateur. He is a skilled professional and was asked to come out of retirement. The blood on the water is that of Secret Service Agent Frank Grady, the most successful anti-assassination Agent in the history of the Secret Service!"

Gathering himself, Secretary Klems continued . . . "It was Agent Frank Grady who recognized and took down Don Pew, who had arrived at a news conference with the intent of assassinating Governor Cross of the State of New York. It was Agent Frank Grady who located and took down Don McKee, the Rogue Secret Service Agent who had already received half of the million dollars promised for the assassination of President Elect Odie Knott.

"Secret Service Agent Don McKee, was considered the most capable and dangerous Agent we had but then he went over to the other side. Agent Frank Grady was taxed to take Don McKee *alive*. He did so. Even after McKee had slashed Max's face to shreds, as ordered, Grady still took Don McKee alive. It is outrageous that you would refer to such a man as an amateur!"

"Yesterday, at approximately 2:15 PM, and less than two hundred yards from where the President stood, Secret Service Agents apprehended Mr. Adali Sims, a professional Assassin. This time around, Agent Frank Grady was relieved of the duty of shedding more of his blood and good looks."

The opposition party blustered, "And why was this withheld from us?"

Press Secretary Barry Klems, oozing condescension, said, "What is there about the word secret you don't understand? For a few political sound bites," Secretary Clems raged, "you have compromised the anonymity of Agent Grady. What was the purpose of this? What did you hope to gain?"

Another stumbled on saying, "Why was Max Brauny on the podium with the President?"

"We had concerns. As some of you are aware, as a young man our President had a propensity to engage in physical confrontations. In the event of that propensity being revived, we are reminded that Max Brauny is well-qualified to protect the quarterback."

• • •

Max was amazed. They were alone with President Odie Knott, the most powerful man in the world, and Frank Grady was not intimidated. "I suspect," Frank said, "but I cannot prove, that the location of Adali Sims was known and that they could have been taken him down at any time. If I'm right about this, then Max and I were not needed on that stage and my part in the Don McKee affair need never have come to light. So why were we there?"

The President sighed, "Because," he said, "you were needed. Every President who wins a second term inherits a lame-duck congress. This particular lame-duck congress, more so than others, is an opposition party intent on derailing any possible progress, a party intent on proving to the public that the party presently in power can't get the job done. Therefore, the opposition party begins positioning themselves to retake the Presidency four years down the road."

Frank said, "My being there, it blew my cover."

"Your cover was already blown! Reporter Frank Bly already had the story. So far we've been able to stall its release by giving Bly a heads up on other stories, but it's too late now. Your part in the investigation and takedown of Don McKee is at this very moment going to press.

"Those attacks on you and Max for replacing Secret Service Agents have backfired, cast the opposition in a bad light, and positioned me to pass the most far-reaching domestic reforms enacted since the days of Lyndon Johnson. We could possibly have delayed the story's release a little longer, but not forever, and it was good for me that it came out the way that it did.

"My wife, my daughter and I would like to have the two of you join us for dinner."

• • •

The President was seated at the head of the table, the First Lady at the other end, and daughter Cathy Sue sat across the table facing Frank and Max. It takes a lot of food to keep Max going, but even he could not match the President's intake. Cathy Sue, tall and tanned, fortunately, had her mother's looks—not her father's. The President and the First Lady were relaxed as they entertained with amiable banter.

They were served desert.

• • •

The President likes his bourbon, and after the two women departed, he poured out three stiff drinks. "My daughter," he said, "hates crowds. A father longs to see his daughter happily married and giving him grandchildren. But who would be appropriate for my daughter? She's 5 foot 10 inches tall and wants a man strong enough that she may surrender to him. My daughter compares other men to Cut'n Shoot, Dennis Huff, the three of us, and views almost every other man in DC as either a buffoon or a wuss.

"Cut'n Shoot is straight-laced and the most rigid man I ever met. While his wife is dying, her being as rigid and stubborn as Cut'n Shoot, she will take a long time doing it

and there's no way Cut will move away from his dying wife."

• • •

The airports were hell. Frank was not happy having it known he had been the one who had taken down rogue agent Don McKee. He glowered when others approached with their shit-eating smiles. At one point Max laughed and said, "I can't remember the name of that actress who said, 'I vant to be alone."

"It was Greta Garbo," Frank said, "And I can damn well sympathize with her . . . .. I heard some things that niggled my curiosity and it pisses me off that my part in the takedown of Don McKee came out. I asked a few questions about the Adali Sims case. I think we've been used Buddy Boy."

"How?"

"I suspect they were onto Adali Sims right from the beginning and the President's political strategists used us as bait to provoke the opposition to attack and when they did, the President's men launched a counterattack that chewed them up and spit out the pieces. There are no angels in public office—power corrupts them all."

Was Frank right? Max could never be sure.

Chapter Eighteen—The Thespian

Gordy Hanson was no world-beater. Six foot two inches tall, in high school he had turned out for basketball and track. He managed to win some of the mile races, but his winning times were not good enough to win a scholarship. Plus, he wasn't much of a scholar. On graduating HS, he joined the Marines for one tour of duty. Leaving the Marines, he took a job with Miller Armored Transport, and married Margery Haig. She was a tall, plain woman who recognized that she was the smarter of the two. Gordy's employers judged him as reliable and unimaginative.

Not true. Gordie's imagination was about to get him in trouble.

Josie Gilmore, driving by at six PM, saw Gordy drive out the gate of the Miller Armored Transport Yard, stop, get out of his car and lock the gate. Josie had a revelation. Locking the gate like that, there would be no one inside, and therefore, the guard locking up had been left alone in the building. Josie followed when Gordy drove away.

• • •

Two weeks of watching established that Gordy was not too bright. Saturdays Gordy would do a three mile run, mow the lawn, weather the silent contempt of his wife, and drive to Denny's to sit alone at the counter with the sports page, a strawberry waffle, coffee, and peace of mind. Josie, now living under the name Helen Trent, took a seat two stools to the left of Gordy. Ruefully, she said, "The tall, masculine-looking ones always seem to have that wedding-band on their left hand. I wonder, do you do it because you're married or do you do it to discourage girls like me?"

Gordy choked in surprise. Finally, some recognition, some respect. Beneficent, Gordy told his self that he would let her down slowly.

As Helen Trent, Josie said, "I admire you. Others do too or they wouldn't have called on you to guard so much money, but it saddens me to know that you being married, the two of us can never be together."

"I know," Gordy said, "that you would never settle for a shoddy little affair, and in order for the two of us to be together, I have to make a commitment. Helen, we could run away together."

Looking troubled, Helen said, "How? I'd have to give up my job and you'd lose your job—how would we live?"

Gordy then dropped his surprise. "All that money at Miller's. We could take it with us."

"Gordy, you'd do that for me?"

"I'd do anything for you Helen—and for me too. We deserve to be happy."

Helen's eyes teared up and they kissed.

Gordy said, "We could live in Rio de Janeiro."

"That would be wonderful my love, but wouldn't they be looking for you there?"

"Maybe at first. We probably should stay away from Rio for awhile and let the heat die down."

Helen nodded, "I hear Costa Rico is nice."

"I'll take care of everything so that if anything goes wrong then you're not to blame."

"Gordy, that is so gallant of you. But no way! We're in this together, and we will rise or fall together. Initially, they'll be looking for you, not me, so you need to get out of the country that night. In my job I hear things and I know where you can get a fake passport. You can't take all the money with you so I'll get us a storage locker, you put the money you can't carry in there and I'll send it to you in five-ten pound packages. When the last package is in the mail then

I'll be able to join you. We're going to have a wonderful life together. Someday a book will be written about our perfect love. We're going to be so happy, my love."

• • •

Gordie flew to Mexico City. From there he made his way to Costa Rico. On his arrival and getting settled, he attempted to contact Helen Trent. She wasn't there. Living well, not knowing what had happened and running short of money, he was forced to return to the states. Stepping onto US soil, he was promptly arrested. The storage locker holding the money had been cleaned out and Josie was in the wind.

• • •

On this dark night the Highway Patrol car pulled in behind Josie and hit his siren. Exiting his cruiser, he walked up to the driver's window. A smiling Josie rolled down the window and said, "What's wrong Officer?"
 "One of your taillights is out. I'm not citing you but you need to get that replaced."
"Thank you Officer, I didn't know, and I will."
When the Officer turned to return to his cruiser he became curious about what was under the blanket on the floor of the back seat. He did not see the revolver in Josie's right hand and she shot him twice and sped away. Fortunately, Josie was not a good shot and the Patrolman survived his wounds.

• • •

Max had closed down careers in baseball and football, moved from sought-after hero to hated pariah and then back to sought-after hero and now retired. What's next? Bernie Blare was still his agent. "Bernie," he said, "find me an acting job."
Tuesday, Bernie flew to New York.
Friday, Bernie called, "Max," he said, "catch the next available flight to New York. Your reservation is at the Wellington. They'll notify me when you get here. Okay?"
"Okay."
The show was tentatively named 'The Squad.' TV Producer

Paul Borucki was interviewing actors in his office, one at a time, for roles as detectives. Jill Miller was to cue Max with a one-liner saying, "This is a bad one."

When Max had Barucki's attention, he said, "That is melodrama. Cueing me with 'This is a bad one,' and me responding, 'They're all bad' is crappy melodrama. It's been done a thousand times and I'm not interested."

Borucki nodded, "What do you see so far?"

"Raw emotion. No nuances, no objectivity, steriotypes, no change of pace, no humor, no thought. I'm ready to pack it in and fly back to Seattle."

Baruchi's eyes lit up. He nodded.

• • •

The actor tentatively chosen for the series lead, a lean and good-looking guy, was over-dramatizing his rage at the offender, what Barucki called 'riding the action,' and he saw his character as a romantic lead . . . plus, he was pushing his script demands. Barucki had enough of his attitude and quietly said, "You're through! Get the hell out of my office!"

Manny Armstrong was six feet five inches tall, long-legged, weighed in at 250 pounds, older than Max, was a black and handsome man who had distinguished himself in the part of Othello. He was being considered for the part of pimp Sweet Daddy Whitman. Baruchi said, "Manny, you're the stereotype, tall, black and handsome, what we expect to see in a successful pimp. Maybe we should break that mold."

Turning, Baruchi said, "Max, I talked to your acting teacher Reginald McNally. Reggie said you're a fine Shakespearian actor. You think you could bring it off as a successful pimp?"

"I'm not what you would expect to see in a successful pimp."

"That is true enough," Baruchi said, "But what if we put your broad figure in a vermillion tank top, girls and gold chains hanging around your neck, diamond rings on your fingers, and diamond studs in your ears? Max, you're not the ugliest guy around but you'll do. You have a sly and knowing look. I think you could bring off the role of pimp Sweet Daddy Whitman?"

"Only if those cast as my ladies, in contrast to me, are tall and elegant. I'd need to get my ears pierced, diamond studs, and let my hair grow."

"For the pilot we'd fit you up with a wig. Depending on how well your part goes over, we could bring your character back for other segments."

"My agent's new to the business so try not to take advantage of him."

"Manny," Borucki said, "You're being cast as 'The Bishop' our lead Detective. You're a strong enough actor to carry the lead." Looking to actress Jill Miller he said, "Jill, you're an athletic white woman with an angel face. You think you can bring off the lean, mean, fighting machine who does not hesitate to blackjack someone?"

Jill's eyes went cold. She growled, "I was a white girl growing up on Chicago's tough south side." Her eyes threw sparks, "What you think asshole?"

Borucki nodded, "I think you can bring it off." Jill smiled, Borucki smiled, and Manny and Max looked at each other and grinned.

• • •

Scene One

The first episode had Detective Dayna Stone, played by Jill Miller, tall and elegant appearing until she opened her mouth and toughed-talked. She had been on Patrol and was being reassigned to Robbery Homicide. The Captain welcomed her and introduced her to the squad.

Then the Captain said, "Now listen up people. We have a citizen from Winnemucca, Nevada, who claims that, *for no reason*, an ugly, muscle-bound, short white man, maybe 250 pounds, richly dressed and with gold chains around his neck and diamond studs in his ears, and with long wavy hair. He manhandled the citizen, spun the citizen, ripped the back of the citizen's coat open all the way up to his collar, and took all the citizen's cash and credit cards."

Heads nodded. One of them said, "Sweet Daddy Whitman. The citizen tried to rip off one of his whores." Someone else muttered, "Big mistake."

The Captain said, "Who's up?"

Every head dropped.

The Captain said, "Stony, this is your collar. Here's his file. Read it and then go bring him in."

Scene Two

Detective Stone didn't bother to knock. She barged right in and threw the file on the Captain's desk. "Captain, I read the file. Sweet Daddy has a habit of putting arresting officers in the hospital. Having me going alone to arrest Sweet Daddy, is this your way of getting rid of me? Cause if it is, *it ain't gonna work!*"

The Captain, coat off, in suspenders and belt, bald headed, leaned back, hands behind his head and said, "You're new Detective, so I wouldn't have let you out of the Station alone. We needed finding out what you're made of. You're going to be partnered up with The Bishop."

Scene Three

"Sweet Daddy, The Bishop said, You're the biggest, baddest white dude around, and me, I'm the biggest and baddest black dude around. We tangle and one of us, maybe both of us, are hospital bound. We have a white sister here, made Detective today. The Squad is screwing her around, saying she had to come out here alone and bring you in. Would you mind screwing with them, have her do that, bring you in alone? You'd make bail in an hour and you know the citizen won't testify because he doesn't want the good folks of Winnemucca to find out he tried to rip off a hooker. It might be days before the Squad wises up."

As Sweet Daddy, Max's eyes, grew big and he laughed. "A cop with a sense of humor. Damn! I like this!"

• • •

In the last scene, as his character Sweet Daddy makes bail and comes out on the Courthouse steps, Stony sees Max and says, "Sweet Daddy, your sheet says you beat up on policemen. Yet you went along with us peaceful. Was that because The Bishop was there? How come?"

"You two were respectful. Those other two assholes started whipping up on me with blackjacks so I whipped their asses good.

You hurt Sweet Daddy or his girls and Sweet Daddy hurts you. You treat Sweet Daddy right, you treat his girls right, and Sweet Daddy treats you right."

As Sweet Daddy, Max looked Detective Stony up and down and said, "This police thing—this not work out for you—You got some real treasures under there girl, so you ever decide you want to make some real bread— you come to Sweet Daddy. I'll see that people treat you right."

"I know you would Sweet Daddy—I know you would."

• • •

The writers and Max went out for Thai food and to kick around script ideas. The girl that seated them was tiny and looked familiar—Max knew he had seen her before—but where?

Max dropped money on the table and got up to leave. The cashier, that tiny creature who had seated them, jumped in front of Max saying, "Where you think you go big boy? You see this fist? You pay now, or wham! I knock you down!"

Then it dawned on Max. She was that same tiny creature, no longer a child, who had accosted him in Thailand and said, "I shine your shoes, suck your cock same time."

Walt spoke up then. "I'll be picking up his bill." Walt and Max looked at each other.

"She does have chutzpah," Walt said, "We could write her in."

The part they came up with was that Dao was an orphaned Thai kid in denims, which she really was, and with a baseball cap and a shoeshine box. Dao still knew how to keep that shoeshine rag popping and was added to the cast as a Broadway character who heard, saw, and knew everything going on in the Broadway strip.

Mathew Koren was then added to the cast as the character Breadcrust Johnny. Mathew was known primarily as a Shakespearean actor, had played Iago opposite Manny Armstrong's Othello.

Breadcrust was a hustler, a real artist, leaving dried crusts of bread in entranceways, retracing his steps, wearing a threadbare but immaculately clean sports jacket, and looking starved. When an out-of-towner grew close to one of Johnny's breadcrusts, he would pick up the breadcrust and begin eating it. Sometimes the out-of-towners would get into competition to see who was giving the most money. Breadcrust was cast as one of Stony's snitches and as an inveterate horse-player. Mathew Koren said, "This is not Shakespeare but it pays a hell of a lot better."

They brought Max's Sweet Daddy character back every third or fourth segment, and the show and it's characters were a success.

• • •

In a later segment, to get a look into a second-story window, Stony kicks off her pumps, The Bishop takes hold of Stony's feet, and with her legs spread wide and her hands walking up the side of the building, he hoists her up to arms length above his head. She signaled to be let down, said, "I got a good look. He's in there, along with two other guys." Then with a sideways glance, she says, "What about you, you manage to get a good look up my dress?"

"You kidding? I'm in love." Stony makes a fist and pushes it slowly against The Bishop's's face. In slow motion, grinning, he pantomimes his head spinning away.

Producer Buruchi said, "That's the key. The Bishop is turned on to Stony, who wouldn't be, she's turned on to him, but neither of them will make the move. Also, Sweet Daddy's in the mix. Let the audience keep coming back in anticipation of one of them coming on to the other.

"Sexual tension is the gas that will keep this show running. Either of you guys make a move on Stony, or Stony make a move on either of you—might be a good moment, but the show would run out of gas. This show will keep running as long as we can keep that sexual tension."

Chapter Nineteen—Max is Shot

Max awoke in a hospital bed in the Intensive Care Unit. Damn he hurt. He was attached to monitors checking blood pressure, checking everything, and had tubes running into his arms and one up his nose.

A white-coated doctor, came in, shined a light in Max's eyes, said, "You remember what happened?"

"Too damn well."

"You think you could talk to a cop about it now?"

"They get the gal shot me?"

"I don't think so. You appear to be stable, and definitely, they want to talk to you."

"How bad was I hit?"

"Twice in the abdomen. It could have been worse. You lost a lot of blood before we got to you but now your vital signs are looking pretty good. Still, we're going to keep you hooked up a little longer. You up to giving the Police a statement?"

"Okay."

• • •

"I'm Detective Malloy. Do you know who shot you?"

"Josie Gilmore."

"Why?"

"We were teenagers when I stopped buying her cons. She said I ruined her High School years, I've always known she was a real bitch. This time around I realize she's a stone psychopath and she started shooting. I'm hard to miss. I reached out for her but being shot my legs wouldn't work and she got away from me."

. . .

Writer Ray Hunter headed for the desk of City Editor Roy Cundiff. "I have something," Hunter said, "it's big."
"What?"
"The shooting of Max Brauny—I have pictures."
"Sweet Jesus."
"Yeah. I was watching when Max finished his run around the reservoir. Max is newsworthy so I followed when he headed for Fifth Avenue. He spotted this good looking woman. She was evidently waiting for him. He didn't look pleased, more like curious, on seeing her. I was sneaking pictures of her and Max when she shot him three times. I think one shot missed. I have the photo's with me now."
"You have them with you?"
"I do. I saw him reaching for her but she backed away and he fell. People were screaming, one guy was already calling 911, so I followed her down into the subway and into the Subway car. She jumped back off just before the doors closed and I lost her."
"Follow me. Cundiff took off in a clumsy lope."

. . .

Max thought he must have been out for a moment. When he came to, he saw an overweight Lieutenant McGinty, someone usually desk bound, and it showed. He was out in the hallway and hopping from one foot to the other.
Surgeon Zimmerman reported, "The surgery went smoothly. More than two inches of abdominal muscle, more than I've seen before, took up some of the shock. "

. . .

A week later, Max received a visit from FBI Agent Bass. "We showed Gordy Hanson the photo's of the woman who shot you. He said she was the woman he knew as Helen Trent."

"I read about the case. Josie Gilmore. The cons she ran on that Gordy Hanson character felt familiar. She tried them on me back in High School. Nineteen years old, she was arrested for one of her scams, conned the Courts into giving her a house arrest plan and a delayed sentencing, and then she split. The judge who made that Delayed Sentencing was not the first to be conned by that little lady. She bled me some but compared to those guys I was getting off light— right up to the day she shot me."

• • •

Ray Hunter visited Max in the hospital. Max said, "You the one took the pictures?"

"Yup. That was me. I always travel with a miniature camera and a voice recorder. I didn't get close enough to record anything said, but I got pictures."

Detective Horace Malloy put his hands together, said, "Max, we know Josie Gilmore was in on the armored car ripoff. You have any thoughts about the money?"

"None."

• • •

On his hospital release, Max took a cab from Bellevue Hospital to the corner of Broadway and Canal, walked south on Broadway to 26 Central Plaza, and took the elevator to FBI Headquarters on the 23rd floor.

FBI Agent Dee Dixon is black, beautiful, and good. Max knew her well. Early in her career she and Frank Grady had successfully worked on a high-profile case. When Dee's assignments take her to the Seattle area, she sometimes spends the night in Frank's home.

It is well known that, whatever the assignment, Agent Dee Dixon delivers."

• • •

Ray Hunter exited the Conference Room—then Max entered. Dee arose from her chair, joined hands with him, and they lip-pecked each other. This breach of the expectable FBI protocol startled the other agents. Agent Torgeson cleared his throat and said, "Evidently the two of you know each other."

Taking her seat and again being all business, Dee said, "Well but not intimately."

"Max, we received a report that you were observed having a meeting with Josie Gilmore on the east side of Central Park —and that you huddled together like co-conspirators."

Max nodded. "I was coming out of the Park when I saw Josie. Last time I saw her we were teenagers."

Agent Torgerson, looking skeptical, cleared his throat.

Not even looking in Torgerson's direction Max said, "Asshole! I'm the one originally tipped off the FBI about Josie Gilmore. Check it out. Reading about the Miller Armored Transport robbery, I recognized that the cons run on Guard Gordy Hanson felt familiar, and then I saw the police sketch. That's when I called the FBI." Turning back to Agent Torgerson, Max said, "You're a real asshole."

Sighing, Dee said, "Agreed." Dee then turned to Max and said, "How did the meeting come about?"

"I had finished my laps around the reservoir when I recognized Josie waiting for me. I said: Josie Gilmore—haven't seen you since high school—."

She nodded, "I've been following your career. You've been busy; Pro baseball, Pro football, a TV series . . . you have regrets about any of that?"

"That's like asking a slut if she regrets having had partners."

"You never did make out with me or my sister. Did you make out with anyone back in High School?"

"You're playing with me. What do you want?"

"This is what I do. It's fun playing with people's heads. Max, you wrecked my High School years. I owe you for that."

"And that was when she shot me—two to the body. I reached for her, she stepped back, my leg weren't working and I fell. Her third shot singed my ear."

• • •

On exiting the FBI offices Max took another look at the seated

Ray Hunter who grinned and said, "You're still trying to remember where you knew me."

Max nodded . . . I know the face but from where?"

"I pitched against you in Triple A. You got two hits off me; sent me back to Double A. That was when I switched to being a writer."

Chapter Twenty—The Secret Service

Max took his friends Miff and Gert, along with their daughter Marsha, out for dinner. Then they returned to 72 Bank. Marsha excused herself to return to her studies, and the three adults got moderately drunk, something each of them did rarely. At some point Gert said, "You are an uncommon appearing man but your heart belongs to the common man. I know this."

"How can you be sure?"

"Because I know the human heart. You love the language of Shakespeare even though you recognize the inherent elitism. In Shakespearian plays, thousands of the common man are sacrificed to avenge the death or even the honor of one of the elite. In all the epic poems through history, (songs, as Walt Whitman called them) up to and including those of Shakespeare, the hero is always one of the elite, a God, and the common man is only cannon fodder. Walt Whitman recognized that William Shakespeare was a common man, while his plays were written from the frame of reference of an elitist. Ergo, Whitman suspected that the Shakespearian plays were not the genius of William Shakespeare, but the genius of a member of the ruling class."

Whitman said 'I will sing the song of the common man, the divine average.'"

"Critics referred to this as Walt Whitman's slop bucket. Max,"

Gert said, "read Whitman. He's our greatest American poet."

• • •

Back when President Odie Knott was a college senior, an All-American football hero, and still weighed only 280 pounds, he had been riding in his girlfriend's car when he saw Pamela Morrow, a black classmate, come staggering out of a bar. Odie didn't think she was drunk and ordered, "Stop the car!" He bailed out. "Pamela, What's going on?"

"Those bastards raped me."

"Which ones?"

"All of them."

Odie ordered his girlfriend, "Get this girl to the hospital and notify the police!" He then waded in, took a few hits from pool cues, slapped the girl's six assailants around, and had them ready to be scooped up when the police arrived.

Odie said, "I think I left my cap in there. Give me a minute to find my cap." He walked back into the bar, flattened the bartender who allowed the rapes to go on, picked up his cap, came out and said, "Okay, I'm ready to go."

Graduating with a 4.0 GPA, rather than pursue a career in professional football, Odie Knott turned to politics. Black and Spanish voters of the state of Florida never forgot that Odie had stood up for Pamela Morrow.

• • •

The Secret Service received a report that Huck Godsey had stated that what President Odie Knott had done was rotten, that Pamela Marrow was black and had no business going into that bar, that Odie Knott had sent her in there and then he came along, saw to it that Huck's son and five other decent white boys were arrested and imprisoned for a rape that never happened. He stated that Odie Knott had done this to win the black and Spanish vote.

"That's all it was" Huck Godsey said, "A cheap political trick. My son was killed in that hell-hole Odie Knott condemned him to. His turn is coming. Soon he'll know the grief of losing an innocent child."

The Secret Service went looking for Huck Godsey. He had sold his farm, cashed out his bank account, and disappeared.

• • •

Because Max was newsworthy, he was asked to assume the role of the Trojan Horse.

The Secret Service, looking to set up a safe house, did a whirlwind tour of, an area Max liked, properties along the West Shore of Hood Canal. The decline from Highway 101 to the Hood Canal shore, in places, is severe. They found a luxury home hidden partway down a steep decline and midway between Hoodsport and Brinnon. The home was shielded by evergreen trees, two large maples, and flowering wild rhododendrons.

It became known that the Secret Service had purchased the property in Max's name, and since his every move seems newsworthy, the media duly reported that Max had installed a state of the art electronically operated gate and that the dilapidated dock was being rebuilt by a team of local contractors.

What remained secret was that there were security cameras everywhere.

Max took up residence, along with Secret Service Agents Dennis Huff and Artie Smith. Townspeople soon took note that Secret Service personnel did the grocery shopping and speculations arose that Max was sheltering the President's daughter. In truth, Cathy Sue was 3,000 miles away.

It worked. Huck Godsey came at night, having discovered, he thought, where the President's daughter was being hidden. Coming by water, Godsey docked his boat and with automatic rifle at the ready, he charged up the stairs looking for someone to shoot. Combat-hardened ex-Marine Officer Dennis Huff was on duty and made no effort to take Huck into custody; he blew Huck Godsey away.

• • •

Max had acquired this secluded property at the price of paying the taxes—it was all too easy—he suspected this gift was not truly free, that in the future favors would be asked. He reasoned that what's free always has its price. So he reimbursed the Federal Government for the property. It seemed like a good idea. It turned out to be a good idea that didn't work.

Chapter Twenty-One—The Landes Art School

"Your average working actor," Max said, "works three months a year. The other nine months he's scrabbling for that three months of work. Life is not always fair, not always easy."

Max's ongoing role as Sweet Daddy Whitman, his celebrity as a baseball and football player, had made Max a 'hot' theatrical property.

Film offers with huge salaries were pouring in, but Max already had big money. The project that interested him was producer Anthony Renner's offer that Max take Macbeth onstage. Renner asked, "Would you be able to work onstage with Fay Rodale?"

"Good question. Could I forget that she called me a fucking freako that should have gone extinct? Admittedly, she's a damn fine actress."

"What about Reginald McNally as the director?"

"Now that I could go for."

• • •

They took the play to Chicago. The show, the other actors, as well as Fay Rodale and Max, received rave revues. Chicago's entire South Side had apparently chipped in to see the show.

• • •

They brought the show back to New York and reopened four

days later. After opening night, backstage, there were tears, hugs and congratulations. Then cast, crew, and spouses traveled on foot to Sardi's. There was much food, much drink, and much optimism, anxiety, hugging, kissing, and nervous laughter while waiting for the reviews. The reviews stated the show was a triumph.

The financial backers were already counting their profit, predicting the show would run for another year, when Max said, "I'll give it six months but then I'll be moving back to Hood Canal. Maybe I'll buy a boat."

Harvey, one of the financial backers, hearing this, smiled his smug little smile and said, "He's angling for more money."

In the silence that followed, Max said, "Asshole! Since you were wise enough to bring up the subject of money, you now have three months to find my replacement."

Maury looked at Harvey and said, "Thank you for that bit of wisdom Harvey, you've always had a knack for screwing up a sure thing."

Fay Rodale, they thought, was strong enough to carry the show, but to replace Max, they settled on Lars Johannson, a pale skinned, tall, and powerfully built Swede. He had never done Shakespeare. Still, he was intelligent, had the passion plus the talent. Director McNally worked with him for two months and it was going to pay off.

• • •

After being replaced as Macbeth, Max went on the David Seaton Late-Night TV Show. Seaton was good, had done his homework, and drudged up some of Max's fonder moments in baseball. He said, "That time in the Mets game. I saw you come up to the plate and bat left-handed against a left-handed pitcher. Did you do that often?"

Max shook his head. "Only that one time."

"And you hit it off the back wall."

"Arnie was fading, he was losing control of his pitches. They were going to walk me while they warmed up his relief pitcher. I always bat right-handed against left-handed pitching. Seeing me step up to the plate batting left-handed, Arnie thought I had confused myself and he took a little off the pitch and tried to slip a fastball down the middle. I wasn't confused, and rode it out for two runs batted in."

"Well this solves one mystery. Pretty tricky. There was talk before your ouster that you might be the next batter to hit for a 400 Batting Average."

Max shook his head. "Nobody ever worked harder than me. I suspect Ty Cobb worked just as hard, but no matter how hard I worked, I was never going to hit 400."

"You were exiled from baseball, and then you were exonerated—so why didn't you return to baseball?"

"I was too raw. Every day I would be looking into the faces of teammates who had signed that restraining order. There was that along with other things I won't talk about.

"Think about it. The stress of breaking baseball's color line killed Jacky Robinson at age fifty-two. Jacky Robinson died and left his family abandoned. I don't want that for my family."

"Would it be acceptable at some later date?"

Max shook his head. "It's too late for that. I'd never get that edge back."

"So now you've abandoned baseball, quit football, done a TV series with Jill Miller, and the play Macbeth with Fay Rodale. Rumors have been rampant about your relationship with Fay Rodale. How will your leaving the show affect your and Fay's relationship?"

"I have to say one thing. Fay is a great actress, a beautiful lady, I love being onstage with her, but she has this one little habit she will not give up . . . and it really bothers me."

Eyebrows raised, David asked. "And what was that?"

Max hung his head and said, "She keeps saying no!"

• • •

Fay called. "Max, thank you so much. Already owing you like I do, you saying that I kept turning you down has kicked my reputation up a notch, made me what is known as a 'hot' theatrical property, and I thank you for that."

• • •

Dean Eve Renard of the Landes School for the Arts gave Max a call. She said, "You're now residing in this area, have you ever considered teaching?"

"Now that's an interesting thought. Tell me more."

"We're a small Women's Art School, our auditorium and stage are woefully inadequate and we are struggling to stay alive."

"Uh huh! You would possibly want my help but you're suspicious. You think I might view the Landes School as a happy hunting ground."

"Sir, you are scaring the hell out of me. As you have said, that is our dilemma. Association with you, with your prominence as an actor, would enhance our academic standing, yet any hint of scandal would be our death knell. It is well publicized that you are friends with the libertine Frank Grady, and that your mother had been associated with organized crime figures. That being said, this school is tottering on the edge of an abyss. Would you be willing to travel here for an interview?"

"You're looking for my help and you ask me to come to you. At the moment, I'm enjoying being out of the limelight. Port Townsend is a small town so maybe that light might be less glaring—something to think about."

• • •

Driving to picturesque Port Townsend, Max stopped at the Blue Moose Café to sample coffee and soak up the local ambience. Then he called Dean Eve Renard.

Max met with the Landes Art School's teaching staff. Dean Renard said, "We're a small Art School in a small community. This is a liberal community but even so, the wisdom of associating ourselves with someone with your notoriety and your stature could raise questions. Shall we begin?"

Jim Ross, the writing instructor, said, "I'm sure with your background you could find many of the larger Universities eager to hire you."

"I believe so."

"So why are you here?"

"Two things. One, my life, up to now, has been intense. I could use some mellow time. I've inherited money, earned even more, I'm tired, I like living in this area, and I received a call from Eve Renard. I'm curious to find out what she has in mind. I suspect she's being honest with me."

"If, as you indicate, you desire the calm of a rural setting, why did you become an actor?"

"That should be obvious. It gives me the break I need from being Max Brauny."

Jim nodded, looked to Enid Hayden who taught modern dance and said, "I'm done for now."

Art instructor Elinore Gibbs said, "I saw David Seaton's interview of you on TV. I chuckled along with Seaton when you said Fay Rodale had that one distressing habit: That she kept saying no. I laughed then, but I'm not laughing now."

"Why did you laugh?"

"Are you attacking me Sir?"

"I'm asking you to think about the technique of acting. Seeing me, most don't feel like laughing; I'm not funny. To get the laugh I needed to set the stage and hit them with a surprise. Fay Rodale never had the chance to say no, since I never asked . . .. David Seaton and I set that up. We did it because it was good theatre."

"Say no more." Ann Boorstein said, "I'm the acting instructor. You are intimidating sir."

"It's true. Initial acceptance of me is rare while intimidation sometimes inspires a mood that looks very much like acceptance. It's not always easy to tell the difference."

Boorstein nodded. "And perhaps we come on strong to deny that we feel intimidated by you. I'm not as strong as I was and I would welcome cutting back to one or two days a week. How would you deal with the green room, girls in half-dress or undress?"

His eyes rolled. "Avoidance, that's how. Now I have a question. Why are you reaching out to me? Is there a problem?"

"There is." Dean Renard, said, "So now you're interviewing us. Okay then. Plain and simple, we're on the verge of bankruptcy. The father of Edith Landes was a shipping magnet. His daughter inherited his fortune and set up a Fund that has kept the Landes Art School for Women afloat all these years. Unfortunately, the Fund is about tapped out. Next year we must go coed and double our enrollment or the Landes School will be no more."

"So . . . You think my presence could lead to an increase in enrollment?"

"We would hope so."

Jim Ross cleared his throat. He said, "Also, I'm the only male on the staff and I am not intimidating. In the past, the local boys were respectful. The climate has somehow changed, is on the edge of turning ugly. Cars show up, park in front of the school and harass the girls. There are only so many ways into this area and the boys have made a game of it, setting up lookouts with cellphones and notifying the cars when the police are coming. The girls are now under siege."

"The Police?"

They're concerned that there's going to be an incident . . . good boys going bad."

• • •

Four girls were sitting on the lawn when two cars showed up. The girls did something they hadn't done before, they smiled and waved. Max walked up to the second car and said, "Move on out boys."

"The driver said, "Hey! I know you man. You're that dude on TV, that Sweet Daddy dude. We're not moving. Those girls want to talk to us."

Max put the heel of his hands up under the driver's open window frame and rocked the car. "Move it boys," he said, "or I'll roll this car and with you in it."

They peeled out. Then Max walked towards the other car. It peeled out while the girls sang out, "Goodb-y-y-y!"

Chapter Twenty-Two—Love and Marriage

Students had been provided with a copy of JAQUES first entrance in Shakespeare's play, 'As You Like It.'

Max said, "Because of the way I look, as an actor I get all the work I want. Some of you will be of a particular type that is in demand, some of you will be in less demand. Some of you will be talented, some of you less talented. However, what I can say is that if you take the time to learn about the craft of acting, in some capacity, if you organize your life, you will be able to make a living in this business. So let's begin."

He looked to the young woman in front of him. "What's your Name?"

"Mainer,"

"Well Mainer, you have Jaques first entrance in front of you. Twenty three lines. You think you could bring those 23 lines alive?"

"I've tried, but they come out dead."

"So let's see if we can bring the first five lines alive. Stand up and let's hear them."

She stood. "A fool, a fool! I met a fool i' the forest,
A motley fool. A miserable world!
As I do live by food, I met a fool,
Who laid him down and basked him in the sun,
And railed on Lady Fortune in good terms,"

"You're right Mainor, the words are pretty dead, not believable. Let's see if we can revive them. What do the words mean?"

"I don't understand?"

"What's a fool Mainor?"

"A clown. Someone whose job is to amuse the Lords at the castle table."

"So, ask yourself, what is this clown doing in the forest? he's supposed to be amusing the Lords at the castle table, so what the hell is he doing lying in the forest?"

Mainor said, "That's what I'd like to know."

"So you're baffled at seeing him in the forest. So play your bafflement. Give us those first lines again."

Mainor did, looked and sounded astonished, and the lines came alive. Max then turned to Susan (who he thought looked troubled) and directed her to give them the first two lines. She did.

"A fool, a fool! I met a fool i' the forest,
A motley fool. A miserable world!"

Max said, "So tell us Susan, what's a motley fool and why does Jaques think this is a miserable world?"

"Motley is the clown dress the fool wears and Jaques hates, as does the motley fool, his being stuck out here in this miserable forest."

Max had won his first battle as a teacher.

• • •

Dean Renard said, "Max, you're a single guy, you have money, you live alone, and you've been cast in the role of pimp Sweet Daddy Whitman. You live in a world where possible entrapment lurks around every corner."

He nodded. "Some of the students are drama-queens. Therefore it's necessary for me to develop strategies for dealing with the student's personal issues while not getting personal. I've developed a series of lectures tailored to ricochet off the class and hit the student or students where they live. I love ricochet shots."

"Give me an example."

"I had two students in mind when I developed my casting couch lecture. Bobbie Betz is serious about coming-on as our sexiest student and I think of her as Bobby-with-the-boobies or as Bobbie Booby. The other, Nonnie Pierson, sparkles on-stage, while off-stage her manner is pleasant but after a time you realized she isn't really there. Once in a great while she will get bratty. Those are about he only times off-stage when she feels real to me. Then she turns unreal again and apologizes for being bratty.

"I'm awfully tired of Bobby Booby's posing for me. Dean Renard, I would like you to sit in on my next class.

"Why?" she said.

"I want you there when I address the topic of the casting couch."

"What if I'm not there?"

"Then I won't touch the topic."

"Max, plain and simple, that's blackmail." Dean Renard then raised her hands up in surrender and said, "OK, OK, I'll be there."

• • •

"Class," Max said, "look at yourself and then look at your fellow students. Ask yourselves if there is one or more amongst you too quick to apologize, too quick to say, 'I'm sorry.' I'm going to step out in the hall while you take the time to determine who you think is too quick to say they're sorry.'"

From the hallway Max could hear the laughter and the giggling but it quieted down in about half a minute. They all knew. Max re-entered the room with a grin on his face and said, "Okay, you have a lucky winner?"

A quiet undertone of voices chanted, "Nonnie, Nonnie, Nonnie."

"Nonnie," Max barked, "Go over to that corner and stand with your face in the corner." She did. His bark was harsh, "How does that feel?"

"I'm sorry I" . . . and the class started laughing.

Max's voice softened. "Okay". . . "Come on out of the corner Nonnie. Now, how did it feel standing in that corner?"

"Not good."

"I want you to remember that feeling. Now each of you take a turn standing in that corner and, like Nonnie, get in touch with your own not good feeling." Max's stern tone helped install that not good feeling. Then his manner softened. "I want each of you to remember that feeling if you start to apologize when no apology is warranted. There are sharks in the theatre world—and they can smell the aroma of someone, male or female, willing to efface themselves." Max turned to the class and said, "You've all heard of the casting couch. Suppose you're up for a part and the producer, the director, or the leading actor starts coming on to you, hints you could get the part. What does that tell you?" They looked uneasy, eyes shifted as they looked to each other. Max said—"That tells you nothing—if you actually get the part after sleeping with them it was because you were the first choice all along. If you were a close second and the first choice has turned down the casting couch, do you actually think that a roll in the hay will transform you into the first choice?" There were murmurs and an uneasy shifting of eyes. Max's tone again softened. He said, "It may—maybe one time in a hundred—and those, my friends, are damn poor odds. But, even if you got the part you've also established your reputation as a trick. Flat out, professionally, it's not worth it."

"If you're the first choice all along they may still approach you for a roll in the hay, and if you turn them down in a way that doesn't embarrass them, the odds are that ninety nine times out of a hundred you'll still get the part."

Bobbie Betz, the one he thought of as Bobbie Booby, challenged Max on that. She said, "How can you be so sure?"

"I'm a star of stage and TV. When I leave this rural area, I break bread with other stars and we all know that being a trick, fucking for parts, doesn't work. One actor I know likes to collect tricks he calls his boobies. They come on to him or he comes on to them saying he will help them break into the business. After he screws the boobie, he rises from the bed, goes into the bathroom, and out of the bathroom comes his agent. One of these days, an outraged father, brother, someone, may shoot that bastard, but it won't be one of the boobies because, male or female, it doesn't matter, once a booby, a trick, always a trick."

Bobby Betz blew off the lecture while the others, *probably all the others*, he thought, had heard him.

• • •

Laura Warren called. "Max," she said, "Can I come and see you?"

"There's a decent restaurant in Brinnen. That's on the west side of Hood Canal. Call me when you get there."

She did.

When Max arrived, Laura had already paid her bill, was sitting in her car with the door open. Every time he'd seen Laura, the meeting had been emotional, tense. This time Max drove up beside her, and the meeting was calm, warm, and he thought, *something has changed.* They spoke briefly, and then she closed the car door, started her engine, and followed Max as he drove off.

Electronically, Max opened the gate, they parked, he closed the gate, and Laura went for a walk through his home and property. Out on the veranda, she stared down the steep incline to Hood Canal, then turned and said, "It's time for me to confess."

He stepped back, gave her room and said, "Okay."

"Much of my work is as an illustrator doing character sketches of public figures. It pays well. One of my tricks as an illustrator is to recognize that most faces are slightly asymmetrical and that usually goes unnoticed. An exaggeration of that asymmetry, one eye or ear lower than the other, to exaggerate the asymmetry others would not consciously recognize, is part of my technique. Your head and face are quite different, but symmetrical. Seeing that fascinated me."

"Uh huh. So why are you telling me this?"

She sighed, "Buying time. When I first saw you I stared at your crotch. I was curious, were you as heavy down there as you were everywhere else? Then you looked in my direction and I locked eyes with you and my eyes stayed locked on you face so you wouldn't catch me staring at your crotch.

"Dad told me that women liked going to bed with you . . . what they didn't like was others knowing that they were sleeping with someone as different as you."

"What about you?"

"Me too. That was the way it was for me then, but not anymore. Max, you've wanted me for a long time. I admire you, you took care of me when I was sick, and I'm yours if you want me."

He kissed her and picked her up, "You sure of this?"

"I want this to work. I'm not frightened of you Max, but I'm frightened of me. Can this work? I don't know."

She laid her head on his chest, and he carried her up and into the bedroom. Without speaking, they got undressed. He then gently laid her on the bed and said, 'There's a lubricant in that bedside table.'"

· · ·

Midnight, the windows were open and they could see moon light reflected on the waters of Hood Canal. They were very still with Laura atop Max and with her face on his chest. She arose from the bed and entered the bathroom. He heard running water. She emerged from the bathroom with a wet washrag, slipped between his legs and washed him. Then she took him in her mouth. Shortly, he cautioned her, "The teeth, the teeth, be careful with the teeth."

When she tired, she laid herself beside him and said, "I didn't come to you as a virgin, but I never did this before. If you want this from me then I will learn to do it proper."

They had a quiet wedding in Port Townsend.

Chapter Twenty-Three—Nonnie Pierson

The advertisements for the Landes School of the Arts went out with the teacher's bios and received a favorable response. Dean Renard then marched down to the bank with the torrent of applications for enrollment. A loan to finance the construction of a new and expanded dorm, along with an expansion of the dining hall, was approved. In the meantime the influx of male students would be housed in the dorms at Fort Warden Park.

• • •

FBI Agent Dee Dixon called Max. "A seaplane will be pulling up to your dock in about twenty minutes. We need you Max."

Their flight landed on Lake Union in the heart of Seattle. Dee Dixon met Max on the dock and escorted him into the King County Jail. They entered an interrogation room and young Jack Capper was dumped in the room with them. He had spent the night sleeping in his own vomit. Dee said, "Rough night Jack?"

"You could say that."

Jack had assumed a new identity within the FBI's Witness Protection Program. He was a decent looking young man but with his father's arrest, testimony, and placement in the Witness Protection Program, Jack had fallen into a two-year downhill slide into alcohol. Emotionally and physically, that seventeen year old kid was in poor shape. Only Dee, Laura, and Max were aware that Jack and his father were in the Witness Protection Program.

On the previous night Jack had knocked down a half bottle of Southern Comfort, took off in his father's car, and totaled it.

This was one screwed up kid, but he was intelligent, had a spark, and intuitively, Max liked him. He called Laura. Over the phone, Laura agreed they should take Jack on. Dee came with them when Jack and Max were flown back to Hood Canal. Jack struggled his way up the stairs and Laura said, "Have you eaten?"

He shook his head.

Laura supplied Jack with a terrycloth robe, and steered him into the shower. While he showered Laura did his laundry. Then they sat him down and Laura fed him breakfast. Dee was then flown back to Seattle.

• • •

The west shore of Hood Canal houses a number of recreational parks. Max prefers the Falls View Park. One path from the parking area leads to a lookout point where the waters cascading down may be viewed from above while another pathway leads down to the stream far below. The first time they took that walk down to the stream, on the walk back up, Max stopped several times as Jack fought not to quit—still, he was shaking and stumbling by the time they topped out.

In preparation for the day when the Landes School would go coed and he could enroll, Jack joined with Max on his Falls View walks. Being small boned, he was never going to be a hunk, but what he could be was alert, healthy and moderately attractive. Jack awakened to two facts. One, there were girls in this world, and two, he enjoyed writing. Jim Ross said that Jack had as much natural writing talent as any student he'd ever had. The yet unanswered question was whether he would get his life in order and do the work necessary to become a decent writer. Jim Ross said, "Raw talent goes nowhere without dedication."

• • •

Jack Capper and Nonnie Pierson connected. She was good for

Jack in that she gave him ample opportunity to remind her that she was Nonnie Pierson and not a non-person. In process, he himself established a new persona. His own rejuvenation was underway while Nonnie was giving serious thought about the wisdom of changing her name. Then, decisively, she declared, "I am not a non- person, I am Nonnie Pierson."

• • •

Max received a call from a woman who gave her name as Marge Thompson. She said, "Mister Brauny, I need to talk to someone."

"This is a private number. How did you get it?"

"My niece is one of your students. Her boyfriend dialed your number for me."

"Un huh. You been drinking Marge?"

"My boyfriend and I were drinking and watching Hogtied on the internet. I asked him to tie me up like on Hogtied. He wasn't doing it right, we got in an argument, and he was beating the shit out of me when Nonnie came in with her boyfriend. Jack picked up the bottle and clopped Walt Phipps on the head and Nonnie called 911. Walt is big—Jack threatened to clop Walt again if he tried to get up."

"I'm hearing background noise. Are you at the hospital?"

"We're in the ER."

"Put Jack on the line."

"Hello?"

"Jack. Where do you stand with the police?"

"So far they're okay with me. They just finished taking my statement. Marge has a broken collarbone, bruises on her arms, and a shiner that's a real beaut. I think they're going to keep Marge overnight. Walt Phipps, the guy I clobbered, they say I gave him a concussion. They're keeping him overnight and handcuffed to the bed."

"Jack, you and Nonnie stay put. I'll be there in an hour."

By the time Max arrived Officer Trelawney had finished taking everyone's statement. He said, "Walt seems to think of himself as some kind of a bad dude. He's making threats about what he's going to do when he gets out of here. I do hope you're not planning on convincing him that this might not be a good idea."

"Heaven forbid. Would I do that? It's none of my business. Officer Trelawney, I have a cute little trick I'd like to show you. Do you think you could secure me a couple of forks from the cafeteria?"

. . . "I could do that."

Officer Trelawney returned with two forks. Handing Max one he said, "Show me." Max took the tongs in the palm of his hand and with the rest of the fork standing up and using his thumb as the post, he gave the fork handle a wrap. Then he slipped the loose ring off his thumb and tucked the end of the fork into the center. Officer Trelawney said, "Why did I doubt it. Okay, here's the other fork. Do you think Walt might enjoy seeing that trick?

"Well now, I hadn't thought of that—He just might."

• • •

When Max came out of Walt's room Officer Trelawney was waiting. He said, "I hope you never threatened old Walt."

"Heaven forbid. I would never do that. Though I wouldn't know what he may have been thinking. I don't think he was feeling very good. Usually people smile when I wind that fork around my thumb. Walt didn't smile. Maybe it was because I didn't smile enough."

Trelawney said, "That's probably it. I'm so glad you didn't do anything threatening."

• • •

When Max returned home he made some phone calls.

The next morning, before his first class, Max returned to the hospital. Standing in the hallway, he listened as two AA ladies, both having long-term sobriety and also being longtime members of the Sado/Masochism Community, were telling it like it is. Max's hearing is not great, but standing in the hallway close to Marge's open door, he could catch enough to follow the gist of their message, that drugs and alcohol have no place in the S&M lifestyle. Then they stated that if she wanted to join with them and be introduced to the BDSM (Bondage/Discipline & Sado/Masochism) lifestyle, then the first thing she needed to do was get clean and sober.

Max thought they were doing the right thing. Was Marge listening? . . . he didn't know.

• • •

Dean Eve Renard asked Max to meet with her in her office. He detoured to the staff lounge for coffee and took a seat in front of Eve's desk. She said, "Max, it appears to me that you are by nature a private kind of person."

He sighed. "It's true. I would prefer a more solitary life such as that of a writer or a scholar, to be able to sit in the back row and go unnoticed by all but family. Unfortunately, I have neither the talents for these pursuits nor the option of going unnoticed. The spotlight shines on me whatever I do. The focus of attention even spreads to those around me."

Dean Renard nodded, "That it does. The spotlights focus on your celebrity has spread to include our other teachers as well. Jim Ross has pointed out that while our student population has more than doubled since you came on staff, the queries about his own qualifications have quadrupled."

Enid Hayden concurred. She said, "The queries I received in the past, you could pick up the tone, they had assumed I was some kind of a hack, which is true, etching out a bare living in some backwater school. The queries I now receive have a more respectful tone."

Dean Renard said, "Max, in this rural area the glare of the spotlight spreads to include the others around you."

• • •

The time was growing near and Max moved wife Laura to the maternity ward at the Jefferson County Hospital. Four days later they called and informed him that his wife had gone into labor. He arrived in time to witness the birth of their beautiful baby girl. Definitely, and to his profound relief, she took after her mother and not Max. Laura named their beautiful baby girl Amber.

Chapter Twenty-Four—Kilolo Tshombe

When Huck Godsey invaded the Brauny home it had been Agent Dennis Huff who blew him away. Now Huff revisited them. He said, "We tend to keep an eye on those who serve and have served the President. You had Jack Capper for three months and during that time you aborted the downhill slide the boy had been on for two years. Fortunately, or unfortunately, we've also interviewed your fellow teachers and your students."

"Uh huh. And what do they have to say?"

Huff sighed, shifted his feet, and shook his head. His voice was gruff, muffled. Looking down at the floor as if embarrassed, he took a deep breath and said, "There's no way to say this tactfully so I'll just put it out there." Looking sorrowful he said, "Max . . . they all say they like you, trust you."

Laura let out a gasp and Huff chuckled. "I couldn't resist setting you up and messing with your head. Doctor Kengo Tshombe is a fine man. He's the physician that Frank Grady's deceased wife, Dr. Melina Hamdi, worked with during her time in his homeland. Doctor Tshombe has an inoperable brain tumor and not much time.

"While at their home in Africa, his daughter Kilolo Tshombe hid in the brush when a militant group came searching for her father. She witnessed the marauders drag her mother out of their home and hack her to death with machetes."

Agent Huff continued, "Doctor Kengo Tshombe located his daughter Kilolo, smuggled her out of the country, and brought her to America.

. . .

Doctor Kengo Tshombe, accompanied by his daughter Kilolo, arrived by ambulance.

The carefulness with which Kengo watched how Laura and Max related to his daughter was striking.

Days later, the table having been cleared and dishes put in the dishwasher, Laura, Kengo, and Max gathered in the living room. Kilolo was not present.

Kengo Tshombe said, "My tumor is growing and is inoperable. Shortly I will be unable to care for my daughter. My daughter has already lost her mother. Soon, she will lose her father. "Would you and Laura be willing to adopt my daughter?"

Max looked to Laura. She said, "Being all alone has to be scary for a black African girl in white America." She looked to Max. "You need to do this Max."

"Doctor Tshombe, I can't replace you, but what I can do is protect. Kilolo is a courageous, beautiful child, and it will be an honor to accept Kilolo into our home."

Laura rounded up Kilolo and she arrived bringing the bassinet with little Amber. They lined up silently in front of Kengo and Max.

. . .

"Kilolo," Laura said, "It is your father's wish that after your father is gone you will live with Max and me as a member of this family."

Silently, Kilolo moved to the side of her father and leaned into him— as if holding him in place. She nodded.

. . .

The adoption of Kilolo was finalized. Kengo Tshombe then asked that he be placed in the hospice ward next to the Jefferson County Hospital. Again, Max was witness to the peace that came with surrender. That peace and that courage was an awesome sight.

Watching Kengo Tshombe—once more, Max was reminded that

surrender can be an act of nobility and courage.

• • •

They took Kilolo to see her father the day after he was hospitalized. On entering Doctor Tshombe's hospital room they found the girl's father being addressed by his first name and in a patronizing manner. That offended Max.

Saying, "I want to talk to you," he took the Nurse by the front of his smock and marched him out into the hall and not far from the Nurses Station. He said, "Doctor Tshombe is a distinguished gentleman and a distinguished medical man! He is your superior in every respect and you will not patronize him. You will address him as Dr. Tshombe or as Doctor. I can address him as Kengo because we're friends but you're not his friend. Therefore, you will address him with the courtesy and respect he deserves or you will answer to me! Is that clear?"

"It's clear."

"Good. Glad to hear it." Releasing the Nurse Max took the three steps to the Nurses Station where two wide-eyed Nurses had observed this in silence. He commanded, "You will see to it that Doctor Tshombe is treated with respect." One Nurse responded in a drawn out hushed voice saying . . . "Yes Sir . . .."

• • •

Kilolo was as black as any child they'd ever seen, intelligent, beautiful, well organized, and without learning disabilities.

Agent Huff and Max visited Principal Smiley at the local high school. Learning that Kilolo Tshombe was a survivor of the bloodbath currently going on in Zaire, had witnessed her own mother's beheading, had escaped the same fate by hiding in the jungle, Principle Smiley assured them that every effort would be made to shelter, protect, and keep Kilolo safe.

• • •

Kengo had stated, "When my time comes, so that my spirit will be present, I wish that my ashes be kept in the home during the time Kilolo is growing up."

Kengo also requested that after his daughter grew to maturity, established her own life, his ashes would be returned to the land of his birth and scattered in the wind.

Max was truly humbled. He said, "It will be an honor."

• • •

Each day after school , some days by Max and some days by Laura, Kilolo was taken for a visit with her father Twenty-one days after Kengo entered the hospice, Kilolo's father was alert one moment and gone the next.

• • •

Ebony-complexioned sixteen year old adopted daughter Kilolo had no difficulty with her school studies, even hid in them. Initially, even though she was beautiful, less because she was black but more because she was solemn, she didn't get much attention from the High School boys.

Then Hal Carter came along. He was a big broad-shouldered blond kid who lettered in football and basketball, was popular, pulled down good grades, and took notice of Kilolo. Gradually, then more quickly, Hal was spending more time with her. For a long time, little child Amber and this big teenager Hal Carter were the only two people who could coach a smile out of Kilolo.

Three months later, seeing Hal come out of the cafeteria and with Kilolo hanging on his arm-, another girl commented, "Kilolo, you just walked off with the handsomest, most desirable jock in Port Townsend."

• • •

Hal Carter Sr. and his wife Lois called. Max and family seldom had visitors. On this occasion, when the car pulled up to the gate, Laura opened the gate electronically, they drove in, the gate closed, and Max opened the door to the carport and welcomed Hal Sr., his wife Lois, and their son Hal.

Hal Sr. said, "Our son has stated he is willing to give up an athletic scholarship, if necessary, in order to be with Kilolo. Frankly, my wife and I are frightened for our son. My brother says it's like

Hal's been hypnotized . . . like he's under some kind of a spell."

"I'm glad you're here," looking sharply at Hal, Max said "You've been under a spell allright, one that says everything will be allright. That's bullshit! Nothing is ever allright unless you work for it and sometimes not even then. You've been the lucky recipient of Kilolo's affection but Kilolo comes to me or my wife seeking answers to 'what if' questions. She turns to me or my wife because so far all you do is say that everything will work out. Kilolo is living in a strange new land and she deserves more than wishful thinking!"

Hal Senior's voice had an edge to it. "If something were to happen I'm sure my son would rise to the occasion."

"You think so? Well let's see!" Turning to young Hal, Max said, "Let's see how you rise to this occasion. Unless you and Kilolo together can come up with a list of agreements on how you will deal with each and every contingency, including what if you marry, what if you don't, what if you have one or more children? What if you don't have children? What if you decide this is not working? Hal, you bring me a copy of solid agreements on how the two of you will deal with each and every contingency *by six AM sharp* or I will forbid my daughter having anything more to do with you." Hs voice then rose on high. "You do not want to challenge me on this. I can be quite formidable. How your parents may respond to this is between you and them and that is none of my business." His voice again rose, "but how you relate to Kilolo, that definitely is my business."

Hal Senior looked to his wife and said, "Well, that's clear enough." Slapping his hands on his thighs, he stood, said, "Mother and I are leaving." They were headed for the door when Hal Sr. and Lois turned, looked back and said, "You coming with us Hal?"

Hal paused . . . "No," he said, "I think I'll stay."

Hal Senior and his wife Lois departed and Laura and Max went to bed. The two youngsters were left to work out their agreements.

They awoke twice during the night in response to baby Amber's cries. Both times Kilolo took care of it. The next morning, at six o'clock sharp, two bleary-eyed youngsters presented them with their list of agreements. The list was seventeen pages long. Laura and Max looked it over. Laura said, "They've covered all the bases."

"So they have."

Turning to them, Max said, "This is good. You two have given this a lot of thought.

The only addition I would add to this is never drop your eyes and never apologize for your relationship. And Hal, don't you ever screw up."

He never did.

. . .

Of all the professional undertakings available it appeared to Max that anthropology offered the least employment opportunities and payed the least. Still, that was what the two of them wanted. Did looking at Max pique their interest in anthropology? Max never knew and cared even less.

The University of Montana's Anthropology Department had an excellent reputation. It was decided that when the time came Max would provide the two of them with tuition and living expenses.

Hal was a decent athlete but he decided to skip sports and devote his time to studies and Kilolo.

Chapter Twenty-Five—Peace

Jack surprises Max from time to time. He and Nonnie Pierson had been an item for two years and Nonnie is a dedicated actress who works constantly to get better. Jack Capper, meanwhile, is someone who disappears onstage. However, as a director he knows what he wants and is also the writer/student who inspires Jim Ross as a teacher.

They are not alike, Jim and Max, but they have a chemistry that works. Jim has this student, Jack Capper, who is writing a play about a screwed up teen-aged girl whose family is living within the FBI's Witness Protection Program. Jim works with Jack to refine the script while Max tries out the script in its current form. Max would give different students a shot at different roles. Of course Nonnie Pierson, talented and having grown up in a dysfunctional family, is a natural for the lead, while Jack is a natural for writing the play. Jack spent two years pruning his play to where he didn't cringe on seeing it being enacted.

• • •

Agent Dee Dixon came to see Max. "You got Jack Capper headed down the straight and narrow . . . how did you do it?"

"It was Jack. He saw what he wanted, saw how Laura related to me and he wanted that with Nonnie. Plus, he saw that, more than anything else, he wanted to write.

Max said, "I was a kid with big money after my mother was killed. Why didn't I blow it and end up on Skid Row?"

"Because you had friends and you had character?"

"Wrong. That's the expectable answer. What's true is I knew what I wanted—I was focused. I wanted baseball—and so I never drifted. I think most failures are the product of not being focused, not being clear about what it is you really want. Reginald McNally, my former acting instructor, in what now seemed like another age, had on occasion found it necessary to pull me through an emotional wringer to prepare me for a particular scene. Do I have to do the same with Nonnie Pierson? Definitely not. Give her even a hint of where to go and she's there."

Later, he was to say, "In person Nonnie tends to be shy and withdrawn but when she cuts loose onstage she can tear your heart out.

"Jack has three Plays he's working on. He has something to say—because he is a born writer, couldn't have been anything else, but also, he was writing this one play within his courtship of Nonnie; he wants that girl, and she wants him."

Jack's play opened at The Little Nickel Theatre in Seattle, had a decent run of five weeks. The playwright, the play, and Nonnie as the star, moved to New York and had a decent Off Broadway run. In appearance, Nonnie might not be one's idea of what a leading lady would look like, but damn, she was good.

• • •

Frank Grady called Max and announced that there was someone in his home who wanted to come see him. Max said, "They're going to have a hard time doing it. The rains haven't let up for eleven days and nights, the waters have flooded out Highway 101 to the south, and north of us a hillside has washed down and has 101 blocked. They'd have to come by water."

• • •

Through the rain and in the descending dark Max monitored what appeared to be a Coast Guard craft heading for their dock.

They tied up and a holstered officer stepped out on their dock.

A tall blond woman attired in a raincoat, rain hat and sneakers reached out a hand and the Officer assisted. The two of them began the climb up to the home.

The home had a history. Huck Godsey had also come by water, had come charging up these same steps with an assault rifle at the ready and Secret Service Agent Dennis Huff had blown him away.

When the present intruders reached the top of the stairs Laura, bless her, had already relieved Max of the automatic shotgun. The woman in raincoat, unmistakably, was the President's daughter Cathy Sue. A Chief Petty Officer had followed, dropped the bags and departed.

The Gold Braid said, "The Coast Guard has been assigned to escort this lady to this location." Mission accomplished, he left.

• • •

Cathy Sue was babbling. As gently as he could, Max said, "Cathy Sue, it's time. Cut to the chase."

She swallowed. "Okay. My father wanted me out of Washington. I've been making an ass of myself over Cut'n Shoot."

• • •

Lonny Bean was unloved by everyone including his wife. He professed to be the local authority on Max Brauny even though they'd never met.

Lonny Bean, logger and heavy equipment operator, considered himself a man's man and had been doing his best to stir up community opposition to Max and family, his efforts had garnered him a sparse following while his wife baited him by stating that she was thinking of leaving him and going to live with Max Brauny. That escalated their usual marital uproar. His wife disappeared from their home and Lonny reported that his wife was with Max Brauny and was being detained there against her will.

Max received a call from Chief Hauch demanding that he put Clarice Bean on the line and right now! Max thought, *this man is an idiot,* but what he said was, "I don't think we've ever met the lady and she is definitely not on our premises. You're welcome to come and look for yourself—just don't do anything that will frighten the children."

Chief Hauch blustered some, but declined the invitation. Since Chief Hauch wasn't going to do anything, Lonny Bean put his rifle in his pickup and set out to rescue his wife. Officer Trelawney, always on the ball, intercepted Lonny.

• • •

In lockup overnight, Lonny learned that his wife was staying with a married couple at the Port Townsend Trailer Park. Upon his release, shooting high, Lonny riddled the trailer.

After his release from jail, Lonny and his wife got back together and resumed the discord, the uproar that was their marriage.

Cathy Sue was on her third trip back to DC.

• • •

The drive from the Landes School to Max's home takes about an hour. He enjoyed the drive coming and going the three days a week he taught.

When he arrived home Laura said, "Cathy Sue called. She said that John was holding his wife's hand when she stopped breathing. Cathy Sue will be staying for the funeral and will call when she knows what she wants."

• • •

Cathy Sue called. "Max, Edna's death, in a way, it was a relief—John no longer seeing her so helpless and in pain—it was over. Max, the Memorial Service was dignified and emotional. Cut is doing what he did in football. No matter how injured, how bad he hurts, he keeps on trucking. Seeing his pain is about all I can tolerate right now. We're planning to marry in the Spring. John knows about my hiding out with you and your family. If I need anything I'll call."

• • •

So there you have it. Max's life, up to this point, has been a series of dramatic events. Max has now won a level of acceptance while he remains a private type person.

Walking on Port Townsend's North Shore Beach with his wife and their two daughters, tiny Amber asleep on his shoulder and adopted daughter Kilolo walking arm in arm with wife Laura is a sublime experience. Max didn't miss the drama that's been his life, not one damn bit, he did not expect this quietude to last, that would be unrealistic, but he was enjoying it while it lasts.

143

Chapter Twenty-Six—A Turnaround

Max received a stiff eight by ten envelope in the mail. The return address on the envelope was 7036 50th Avenue NW, Seattle, Wn. That address would have been located somewhere in the middle of Elliot Bay. There was no message. The envelope contained the long missing pictures of Max's mother.

Laura watched as Max, deeply moved, for three days, walked about looking at the pictures of his mother. He said, "Laura, the town of Port Townsend is the most relaxed and accepting of others town I've ever seen. What would you think about us looking at houses in Port Townsend.

She gasped, "Max, as long as I've known you, been with you, you've been a civil man, while also you maintained a splendid isolation . . . you'd give that up? I would welcome us moving into Port Townsend, actually joining the community. I'd be willing to give up this elitism stance we maintain in a heartbeat."

• • •

They purchased a nine room house not far from the grounds of Fort Warden, purchased new rugs, new furniture, moved in and put their Hood Canal property on the market.

Max continued teaching three days a week and along with Laura, the two of them frequently had lunch at the Blue Moose Café.

While the Braunys had always been polite, and still were, there was now something different, more relaxed, more social about them. Social Worker Annie Friedland, a short, dumpy looking woman, but sharp as a tack, had seen Laura arrive at the Blue Moose shortly before Max was due. She approached Laura and said, "Your husband seems different, less guarded, more approachable. Am I wrong?"

"You're not wrong." With a brilliant smile Laura continued, "Small things can have an enormous effect, I won't tell you what, but it was a very good thing that happened."

A day later Annie Friedland knocked on Max's door. When he answered she said, "May I come in?"

"Please do. What's up?"

"Did you hear the fire engines?"

"We did. Everyone okay?"

"Okay but now homeless. Rex, having just got this new job, and still broke and with a wife and three kids and no roof over their heads, their situation is bad."

"Bad but not hopeless," Max said, "Get him to his job, get the wife and kids over here and we'll put them up."

• • •

It became known that when all other sources failed, Social Worker Annie Friedland, only Annie Friedland, could turn to Max Brauny who would ask, "Who to and how much?" Annie would tell him and he would write out the check and sign it.

• • •

"In summary" Max said, "I've had enough drama in my life and have settled down to life as a country Squire, teach three days a week, my wife teaches art three days a week, does her own artwork, and in general we are a part of this community.

THE END